Nowhere Man

(

A mystic

NOWHERE MAN: TRANSPORTER

First edition. July 14, 2019.

Copyright © 2019 Laura Jean Lysander.

ISBN: 978-1393199373

Written by Laura Jean Lysander.

Novel adaption from the Original Screenplay

3rd Edition~

Updated version

By

Laura Jean Lysander

FORWARD

This is an updated version of the second edition. It has more time spent with editing and description.

The idea for this project came to me from a lucid dream I had in the 1990's. It was starkly ominous and stuck to my memory as I awoke up from it, and I jotted down whatever I could remember from the musings of the night. I didn't start it off as a story, but as a true scripted amateur screenplay and I had always thought of it that way. The screenplay version now needs to be massively updated to coincide with this version and when I have the time and patience to forbear that or someone who'd like to work on it with me, I will dive into it.

I placed this aside for years until I had some more time to dedicate to it, for I kept getting stuck on the dialogue and other ideas about it or how to formulate it. It was just seeming "flat" and needed far more dimension and descriptive accents for in the screenplay version everything is cut down and written in a certain tense and I had to convert it manually and laboriously while writing a novel version. Large portions of it I even missed converting and had to go back to correct. It was the last big project I had written, and it was not started when I was a teenager like all the others but in my late twenties. Once again, I had never thought of publishing it, not even in a Novel form.

Finally, after arduously and with many editions of correction I began self-publishing some of my other work independently, and in raw editions. I went through all the jotted notes and adaptions I had of this project and sat down to write out the storyline adaption in case

3

it was "needed" for anything, and because I seemed to be in the right frame of mind to deal with it. It turned out far odder and interesting than I could have ever imagined, in my little personal hobby mind, with a little "help" from the fab four and their immense talent.

I think it never could have been made what it is which is a hundredfold better without the iconic music and legendary spirits, and I am in debt to the imagery it created with this project. I also added another character to it not in the original screenplay, and added more action and incidents inspired by a friend's four-legged best friend. That does not mean this is a highly polished Sci Fi Novel. It sure isn't. It's mostly a sketched storyline of the plot and dialogue of the screenplay project with other inclusions I added to round it out, and that I truly wanted to endeavor to finish one day because it made me laugh, amused me and it had some kind of merit, and so why not?

Since the person having the dream was I, I was struggling, challenging myself, using parts of the real "me" to form some of the female character that resides as the focal point. She the character isn't totally truly I at all, it never could be, but I used what I could regarding the quirkiness and humor of me just to help it along. It was and still is the hardest thing I have done in writing form, to use myself, and parts of what my true emotional reactions would be as the character to do this.

The other main characters were formed by the traits of some acquaintances of mine, and my fancy ridiculously creative thoughts, fantasy imagery researched as well as someone I had always found interesting in the Celebrity world, for in the dream I had that started this idea this individual was the main character as well, so I used the flavor of this person, and I found it strange to finally have a dream with this individual after never dreaming of them at all; I thought the idea and the action I had from the dream was worth building upon because it stuck to me and irked me deeply. It seemed important so I used it.

This Novel is not professionally edited, and some have told me my projects would fair so much better if they were and I wholeheartedly agree. Yet with my meager means it would cost more to do that than I think I would ever make from my work, so until I do and am able to collect the means to have that done, and go over and re-edit it myself please forgive the rough edits and raw work of this piece and bear with me on it. It will most likely be re-edited and polished again to be a much more put together version in the near future when time allows and more imagery surfaces.

The lyrics are interspersed within the piece as well for it to me is also a "musical," so try to listen to the music while you read it if you like to get the real time idea of what it is in reality showing you, if you can. All of my projects are written this way and forgive me if it seems annoying or disturbing, but that's how it was done, and purposely. I was using music and lyrics to help convey the message.

As I mentioned, all of the Characters and story of this Novel are not real, even If I had used pieces of myself and others alive to help form them, they are not real it is a true work of fiction and has not happened anywhere. There are metaphysical, mystic and esoteric instances and beliefs integrated within the project and in no way are they there to sway you into believing them or to think it is the right way for everyone to choose to live. It is there to bring out its full potential and to enhance the simple message out to give; that Love is all we need. Enjoy~

LAURA JEAN LYSANDER

Dedicated to John, Paul, George, and Ringo...
The Beatles,
Mark Hamill,
and
a lovely little dog named Tonic;
For truly I am sure,
a "Nowhere Man"
exists within us all.

In deep gratitude
And special thanks
To the Cover Artist,
Deanna Lynn Miller,
For her amazingly creative artwork,
And her incredible mother,
Lynn Miller,
Who helped with its organization
And
Creation~

Chapter One

No one could have asked for a better day to be in famed Central Park, New York City, especially in the Conservatory gardens. Birds were warbling, squirrels were subtly snickering and snatching someone's honey nuts, and a particular peculiar person had their smart phone up on high in her back uniform pocket when it should have been turned off.

"Here Comes The Sun" was wafting thru all ears around it, brightening the even lovelier day. It was Kalantha Kirby's smart phone, and she had forgotten to turn it off, kind of.

"Here comes the sun (doo doo doo doo)
Here comes the sun, and I say
It's all right
Little darling, it's been a long cold lonely winter
Little darling, it feels like years since it's been here
Here comes the sun
Here comes the sun, and I say
It's all right
Little darling, the smiles returning to the faces
Little darling, it seems like years since it's been here
Here comes the sun
Here comes the sun, and I say
It's all right
Sun, sun, sun, here it comes
Sun, sun, sun, here it comes

Sun, sun, sun, here it comes
Sun, sun, sun, here it comes
Sun, sun, sun, here it comes
Little darling, I feel that ice is slowly melting
Little darling, it seems like years since it's been clear
Here comes the sun
Here comes the sun, and I say
It's all right
Here comes the sun
Here comes the sun, and I say
It's all right
It's all right..."

SUCH A BRIGHT, BEAUTIFUL sunny spring day, one in the only two and a half week period when the double row of trees near the bathhouses in the Conservatory grounds were in full pink-blushed bloom, and the petals were ever so softly starting to flutter down, papering the stone walkway between them with pink nature confetti.

Nannies with strollers were strolling, park personnel were planting and pruning, tourists were taking photos, and strange-clothed, newspaper-reading odd-seeming gents with scrappy, sweet mutty dogs were sitting upon the benches in the mid-day springtime sun and shade.

Shootie and Kalantha, the duo of landscaping park workers on duty at the time and slaving away, were over more towards the fountain, re-planting, weeding, and tending to the flowers and grounds.

Well, it was Kalantha that was primarily working, as always. Shootie was more talking her loud, hysterical mouth out of it. Kalantha was getting a little bit more than dirty, really putting her all into it, her long, brilliant blonde hair up in a ponytail, looped over and shoved under a cap, and her bright, light blue eyes with her salient, intriguing eyebrows were hidden behind mirrored rose colored kitten shade sunglasses.

She never minded, being a hot mess for the flowers were her babies, she loved working for them, watching them grow, watching it all enhance the beauty of the park. Shootie, her work partner, who was a large, lovely African American lady with the color of creamed coffee countenance, catty light brown eyes and full pouty lips, and with intricately braided hair under her cap. She, on the other hand, was doing everything in her power to jokingly get out of doing any work whatsoever, and Kalantha, as said before, she never minded, at all. It was a perfect combination.

Behind them across some hedges and the row of blooming trees, the odd gent Olin Cian sat on a bench with Ringo, his canine companion at his feet. The New York Times newspaper he was "reading" was high up over his head, and you couldn't see his face or torso at all. In fact he was flagrantly hiding behind it, peeping every so often over to stare *secretly...* over at Kalantha.

He had on this rather worn at the edges black baseball cap, clean but seeming very used and old, so old the NY Yankees sewn emblem in front had almost worn off and away and you couldn't figure out if it was a yankees or Mets cap; and you'd see his large, discerning, sparkly dark blue eyes with long lashes and strong eyebrows peep over the top of the newspaper and cap brim every so often, then flick back down; A rather Jauntily handsome fellow, just odd.

A Japanese tourist couple enjoying the day walked past him and his scrappy, sweet, mutty Ringo on purpose, very slowly. Giggling, they were taking photos with their phones of him, noticing him move the paper down to peek over and stare out, then hide back.

They made a pointy gesture towards Olin, staring at his mis-matched clothes, even seeming to ridicule them. He seemed to have on some sort of a Shakespearean jacket or doublet, or...no, could have even been a coachman/horseman livery jacket of very dressy ornament in the 1800's styling, of black and midnight blue crushed velvet, silver pipings and buttons or ornament, an actual lush costume piece. It even looked like a velvet tailed tuxedo vested combo, but they couldn't really figure out just what kind of jacket it was for it was not of this time period at all, and he had underneath it a flowing old flappy, rippled sheer white renaissance shirt, also a costume piece, cinched with a satin blue cummerbund and topped with this funny dark blue velvet bow tie, again not of this time period, not the clip on type for it wrapped around his neck in one long fabric piece and tied in a real bow. He was wearing some old, black faded jeans for his bottoms, rather worn out but clean, and black high top sneakers, the converse brand, also old but in good shape. It seemed to be very strange attire for a walk, let alone a jaunt in the park. But then again this *was* Central Park and oh the things you see and find here...

"The Delecorte Theater is **that way**," The male Japanese tourist chided at him, and pointed behind him, laughing and walking past with his girlfriend, snapping a photo with his selfie stick. He wrote the word "weirdo" in Japanese under it and sent it out on social media to grab out some laughs from his friends back home, figuring he was or must be one of the actors to the theatre in the park on his break, or one of those vagrant clowns who blew up balloons and created magic shows for the kids, but they didn't see any bags with him for his accessories, just the little mutt.

Olin pulled the paper down from his face, peered back and forth, then smiled warmly and acknowledged the couple, nodding to them silently, who then broke out in laughter again at him, passing him by and shaking their heads, moving over to a cart to buy some ice cream. He wasn't homeless or smelled, they thought, wasn't bothering anyone so they didn't call over any cops. He was just an oddball.

Olin glanced down at Ringo, and nodded to him in silence very slightly. Ringo looked up at him and tilted his head, that famous doggie tilt we all love, as if some form of transmuted owner-mutt communication was going on with the peculiar duo.

"**Martha My Dear**" then started to play on Kalantha's smartphone, in her back butt pocket which was one of the songs on her particular playlist which she still hadn't turned off.

"Martha my dear though I spend my days in conversation
Please...
Remember me Martha my love
Don't forget me Martha my dear
Hold your head up you silly girl look what you've done
When you find yourself in the thick of it
Help yourself to a bit of what is all around you
Silly girl.
Take a good look around you
Take a good look you're bound to see
That you and me were meant to be for each other
Silly girl.
Hold your hand out you silly girl see what you've done
When you find yourself in the thick of it
Help yourself to a bit of what is all around you
Silly girl-
Martha my dear you have always been my inspiration
Please
Be good to me Martha my love
Don't forget me Martha my dear..."

RINGO THEN STOOD UP and doggie stretched, his paws padding down on the stone walkway, and he proudly trotted past the Japanese tourist couple with a strange sound of mumbled growling, then it switched to honestly more like tinkling mocking *laughter* coming from him.

The couple stared down at him as he pattered by, confused and baffled, actually wondering if they heard what they thought they did... laughter, from a mutt?

Ringo rounded the bend and made his way towards Kalantha, who was gathering up her gardening tools to take lunch. He came right up to her and just placed his little paw on her knee.

Startled, she turned to look over and down at him, and her eyes lit up, squinting with adoration, staring into Ringo's unusual eyes, one a bright ice blue, the other a pastel lemon yellow. She couldn't figure out what breed he was, maybe a cross between a Jack Russel Terrier, Catahoula leopard dog, or Australian Shepard...maybe even more but he was very cute and curious. A small miracle of the day, she thought. She gave him a soft pat and scratch behind his half-upright flopped over mottled ears before she stood up and stretched her almost bordering on thin, lithe, lean-muscled frame of a body, and started walking with Shootie towards the woman's bathhouse quarters to finish up the shift. Shootie-? She was still slinging one-liners and jokes, mountains of them, ignoring the little pooch.

Ringo steadfastly started following behind them all the way, until he just couldn't follow them anymore as the door closed, then wane-fully made his way back to his mis-matched clothed partner and jumped up on the bench, pawing at his newspaper to get his attention.

Olin's fingerless-gloved hand emerged from behind it, waving a paper money bill. Ringo snatched it in his mouth and made his way over to a hot dog vendor, pawing insistently at his foot. The vendor stared down to him, peculiarly surprised.

Ringo then stood up on his back feet and reached up to give him the bill. And the vendor, he actually took it, staring down at it oddly, shaking his head. The bill had President Obama's face on it, and was a seven-dollar note. He burst out laughing at it all and dug into his cart, taking out a long, watery hot dog and placed it in a bun, handing it gently down towards Ringo.

Ringo grabbed it in his jaws and trotted back over to Olin once more, jumping up on the bench next to him, curling up to enjoy his newly won lunch...

Olin Cian stared outward remotely, peeking secretly from the paper again, his large, spacey eyes scanning the park in front and all about him, at the people smirking mockingly at him and his odd attire.

He could hear another song playing, softly, and right away he marveled at the coincidence if there were any, for he knew there was, and ironically due to his presence being there in the park at that bench and with just a mild, comic thought that it was playing for him, he had a feeling it was just for him of course it was and he grinned to himself in a sad sort of way... for it was **Fool on the Hill...**

"Day after day alone on the hill,
The man with the foolish grin is keeping perfectly still,
But nobody wants to know him,
They can see that he's just a fool,
And he never gives an answer,
But the fool on the hill
Sees the sun going down,
And the eyes in his head,
See the world spinning around.
Well on his way his head in a cloud,
The man of a thousand voices talking perfectly loud
But nobody ever hears him,
Or the sound he appears to make,
And he never seems to notice,
But the fool on the hill ...
Nobody seems to like him
They can tell what he wants to do.
And he never shows his feelings,
But the fool on the hill ..."

Olin Cian sighed, and continued to pretend to read his paper...

Later on that day, a few hours near quitting time, within a gardening storage room near the Conservatory gardens, Kalantha and her colleague Shootie were wrapping up their shift.

Kalantha was in the back of the room, standing and facing a long table full of new seedlings about to be replanted tomorrow. She was tending them and spraying them with mist softly, tenderly, as if they were her own babies, for, she didn't have any. Babies, that is.

Shootie started washing her hands at the work sink, glancing upward warily to her left, for next to her stood a shelf with a full, long collection of Sci-Fi DVDs, books, small superhero figurines, old movies, and comics... some yoga manuals, a plethora of Buddhist, Hindu, Bible interpretations, different types of scripture interpretations and various types of poetry and astronomy textbooks as well. Stacks upon stacks of it all.

*"**Now And Then**"* a rare, unreleased Beatles song started playing upon the speakers of the player on the shelf-

"I know it's true, it's all because of you
And if I make it through, it's all because of you
And now and then, if we must start again
Well we were not sure, that I love you
I don't want to lose you—oh no, no, no
Lose you or abuse you—oh no, no, no, sweet doll
But if you have to go, away
If you have to go...
Now and then, I miss you
Oh now and then, I...
I know it's true to me...
I know it's true, it's all because of you
And if you go away, I know you...
I don't want to lose you—oh no, no, no

Abuse you or confuse you–oh no, no, no, sweet darl'
But if you had to go, away
Well I won't stop you babe
And if you had to go
Well..."

SHOOTIE TOOK A SLY, confounded peek over at all the paraphernalia on the shelf, rolling her eyes and then letting out a bellowing laugh.

"Hey girlfriend, y'all want me to turn this thing off?" She asked to Kalantha, about the music.

Kalantha looked up from the seedlings, fogged in her own botanical baby world.

"Huh? Oh, sure..."

Shootie then shrugged and turned the music down low, squinting, closely examining the menagerie of collectables up on the shelf, then turned her odd gaze back to Kalantha discerningly, scrunching her already heart shaped lips into a pucker.

"*Girlfriend*, don't y'all ever get sick of this? What a stash! Tyrone my man would die for it. Why you keepin' it *here*? Is it for sale? How much?"

"Nope I don't get sick of it. I think... it keeps me sane. Tyrone can borrow from it anytime if he likes. Most of it was given to me as gifts. Everyone seems to like giving me their old stuff. I have it all on digital anyway. That's why I left it all here." Kalantha cheerfully responded, with a small smirk, still engrossed in the seedlings. Shootie still gave Kalantha her 'wack stare'.

"Lookit all of this, all these books and movies, *what for*? You're not collectin' *t'sell* it? Then what is it *for*? Are you searchin' or researchin' a cosplay character for a whatcha wanna call it some kind of weird wild time? Gonna trade it at Comic Con? I don't see any costume threads here. You sure also do a lot of religious research too, don't you? Yer always studyin' somethin' mysterious, or odd; I'm beginning to believe yer life outside this job here has ceased to exist, that someday you'll just *leave* to one of those made up dang places you're always reading about!"

Shootie let out another bellowing laugh after that remark.

"Tyrone and I are ***goin' out*** somewhere, and it's gonna ***be a real hot time***. You know what I mean. He's got a *friend*, ya know, and he'd really *dig* you. Y'all clean up really good, y'know that, don't ya? Y'all honestly can be really pretty, babe material when ya ain't full of, well, ... **this**. This *is* New York City, ya know, and we never sleep and whatever... *You comin'* Kalantha? That's such a strange name. How'd yer parents wind up callin' you **that?**" Shootie shot to her. Kalantha just blinked at her description of herself, real mellow.

"Well, Shootie, My 'parents' were weird researching botanists, studied theology, liked plants, and lived in Hawaii. I'm named after a plant, a Hawaiian flower."

Kalantha made a stifled laugh and continued to squirt the seedlings, oblivious to her workmate's invitation to "party," to have a hot time, and even a bona fide blind date. That's how she just was, almost all of the time, oblivious to that type of interaction or social agenda. She had, on her own and with her parent's back round and degrees in theology, in eastern ways, philosophy, traditions and open mindedness, studied everything she could get her hands on esoterically, textually, mystic and occult-wise, online and off line, just to figure out what life *was about, who she was, why she was here, as we all are.*

Only... she just did it 24/7. It to her was a hobby turned obsession, continually, even with Sci-fi movies and comics. She was and had become an aficionado par excellence geek, yet a very humble one indeed. Instead of getting a Masters and Doctorates degree in theology as her parents had, or one in religious and esoteric studies and becoming a professor or instructor, she just took a Masters degree in Botany along with her theology classes and worked for the NYC Park

Conservation Department here in Central Park. There was nothing strivingly ambitious about her, never thought or wanted to "be somebody".

There was nothing high and mighty about being in the dirt mulching around and hauling it all the time, landscaping or cleaning up other people's thrown garbage. No one even was aware of how much she had studied. She never told anyone.

And here she was, give or take thirty years old, not looking it in great shape and a weird researching theologizing type botanist just like her folks, who were still in Hawaii. Well, originally they were from New York City, but they had moved to Hawaii right before she was born so she wasn't at all pure blood Hawaiian at all, just her name, and her long, bright blonde hair and fair complexion clearly showed such. It was just her flower name that did.

"Ohh, well then a fancy Hawaiian flower name..." Shootie laughed and started gyrating her hips, doing a hula dance and wriggling her hands and arms. She then stared over at the superhero figurines lined up on the shelf. She swiped up a Wolverine and a Luke Skywalker figure, both about an inch high, examining them and giggling, doing a hula dance with them in her hands.

"I'd take you up on your offer Shootie, but I really need to get these little guys done. Work comes first."

Kalantha held up one of the seedlings, very well knowing she was the one who would wind up doing it all... tomorrow, and the next day, and the next...

Shootie just continued to stare at her strangely, holding up the superhero figures, stopping her gyration.

"Y'all gonna wind up meeting him, or something, someone ridiculous, crazy like all this here you have, y'all know that? Yer up to somethin,' gonna dream it all up and have to join their Avengers or Mutant team!"

She pointed to the superhero figures, then to Kalantha.

"Meeting *who?* Up to something? *ME?*" Kalantha voiced, at a loss.

"Some stupid badass sick hero and then you'll really have a mess of a problem, *Really.* All this stuff you study, and *all the time,* in yer own little tiny fantasy crazed world. Um, is something *wrong?* Y'all haven't *talked* to me in a while. Y'all not still mad at me for makin' you finish that entire bulb and daffodil tulip plantin'? Word, I-I didn't mean to, my man Tyrone had this mad Flu and I-

"No, no, I'm *fine,* I'm really fine. It's just the usual, you know me," Kalantha responded, guiltily. She wasn't even thinking of the plantings, surprised and had no idea she even felt that way or how isolated a hermit she had been, and seemed to be towards Shootie.

"I'll leave you to your destiny then...*unfortunately.*" Shootie told to her, in a disappointed tone, placing the figures back on the shelf and shrugging with a pout.

"My *what?*" Kalantha absent-mindedly mumbled, squirting water, still in some perpetual daze.

"Y'all *heard me.* Y'all have a rockin' banging nice time on another comic con planet, or wherever you *end up.* Beware of the dark side, evildoers, villains, nutty caped crusaders and everything else. *I tried,* but you're in too deep with this. See ya, sweets. Remember, *you must not fail*... on savin' the world and ya know it's all... **up to you!**" Shootie yelled out, drying her hands and grabbing her belongings, still laughing loudly in playful mockery as she was leaving the room.

Now alone in the stillness of the gardening room, Kalantha watered the plants silently, and then sighed.

On the shelf with the low music playing, the superhero figurines still stood...and **moved.** The little one inch Luke Skywalker figure tapped the same size Wolverine figure on the shoulder, and the Wolverine whipped around to face him, quickly.

"You know we aren't supposed to do **this** in front of *anyone!* **She's still here!**" The Wolverine whispered.

"I-I know, but I just can't help it. I think it's about time now for her, don't you?" The Luke quietly whispered back, as he opened his light saber up. It hummed as he examined it, scratching his head.

"Yes, it *is*. She's really in for it." The Wolverine whispered, opening his claws to echo the weaponry and swiping them about.

"Watch where you swing those things, show off," the Luke reprimanded, pointing his light saber at him.

"*Sorry,*" The Wolverine gruffly whispered. "You need to turn *that* OFF."

"I'm going to really miss her, mate." The Luke sadly spoke, shutting down his lightsaber.

"Yeah, me too, kid." The Wolverine agreed

"KID? Honestly... doesn't anyone know how *old* I am? You think... she'll come *back*?"

"Yeah, she will. I don't know if for *us,* though. Doubtful on that; But she will. And compared to me, you ARE a kid," The Wolverine quipped back.

"Bye love," The Luke quietly spoke, waving towards Kalantha.

"*Stop that* she'll *see you!*" The Wolverine tensely growled, grabbing Luke's arm down.

"*Fine.* Can't we go *with* her?"

"*No*! How in the world can we do *that?*"

The Luke figure shrugged, and then... made a very mischievous face, as a Jedi would do as if he had *thought, or* had an *idea*, had devised a clever way to do it, to go *with* her. He then reached over to the speakers on the shelf next to him and pressed the button, turned the volume **WAY UP**.

Kalantha, who was still in the back, was finishing her misting and grabbing her backpack, muttering to herself about what Shootie had said to her.

"Life outside the nursery has ceased to exist, eh? Someday I'll just leave to one of those dang places I read about, eh? Very funny; I-you know, Oh Shootie..."

She heard the music on the shelf start to blast on high and jumped, jolted.

"*Weird.*"

Kalantha then ambled back over to the shelf to wash up her hands, and placed her knapsack down on the table near the shelf with all the figurines and books. She then reached over to turn off the blaring music, wondering how it malfunctioned and turned around to grab a paper towel to dry her hands.

Quickly, the Luke figurine grabbed at the Wolverine's arm, and with him, hauled, jumped swiftly into a pocket *into Kalantha's backpack, unseen.*

Kalantha then swiped up her back pack and slid it on, placing her ear buds in her ears as she started to make her way towards the door, taking one more look at the shelf strangely before she left, eyeing it, softly sighing and closing the door behind her, locking it as the two hidden figures high-fived each other, slipping down further into the pocket...

Chapter Two

Kalantha was now off for the day, in a great mood, walking down the tree-lined garden walkway with her music tinkling through the ear buds in her ears. It wasn't sunset yet but the sky was blazing a gorgeous fire-orange purple, which meant it would be warm and or rainy tomorrow. No matter, to her it was just another day after this one.

She hummed and sang to herself, actually dancing a little skip as she slowly walked, drinking in the lovely little pink pastel petals fluttering down from the trees, as if she was having her own individual confetti celebration, and breathed deep, enjoying the serene, natural beauty about her.

She just happened to pass Olin Cian and Ringo... sitting on the park bench. He was *still there,* hiding behind the newspaper, Ringo curled up in his lap. Kalantha didn't even look at him. She was too preoccupied with her music, the song "***Across The Universe***"... and then she thought, as the botanist she was, to just take one more motherly check at the planting she did on the other path before she left the garden.

She was singing out loud, and with the song softly.

"Words are flowing out like
Endless rain into a paper cup
They slither wildly as they slip away across the universe.
Pools of sorrow waves of joy
Are drifting through my opened mind
Possessing and caressing me...

Jai Guru Deva. Om...
Nothing's gonna change my world
Nothing's gonna change my world
Nothing's gonna change my world
Nothing's gonna change my world
Images of broken light, which
Dance before me like a million eyes,
They call me on and on across the universe.
Thoughts meander like a
Restless wind inside a letter box
They tumble blindly as they make their way across the universe....
Jai Guru Deva. Om..."

Kalantha bent down to check on the plantings... and her hand... her hand? HER hand started TO FADE, becomeTRANSPARENT... WITH SOME GOLDEN SPARKLES AROUND IT...?

"Nothing's gonna change my world
Nothing's gonna change my world
Nothing's gonna change my world
Nothing's gonna change my world..."

SHE GASPED, AND *glared down at it-*

Olin Cian was sitting right opposite of her, peeking out from his newspaper, *watching her and what was going on...*

Kalantha shook her hand, she tried to touch it; it started to come back into view once more, to solidify.

"Er-I gotta get back home, too many long hours outside..." she mumbled, thinking her eyes really needed a check up for she thoroughly did not believe what she had just witnessed.

She immediately looked about her to see if anyone had seen what she thought she had just seen. Olin pulled the paper back over his eyes.

Kalantha's hand once more *repeated* its strange action, fading; becoming transparent, little golden sparkle specks around it... then came *back*. She jerkily stood, still stunningly staring at her hand.

"Uh, I definitely have to get back *hand... hallucinations... I mean home, home...*"

Kalantha briskly started walking through the park towards the large, elaborately gated entrance and exit, still glaring down at her hand, almost bolting, thinking she had some form of sunstroke or nerve damage in her eyes...maybe a bad reaction to the plant fertilizer?

"Sounds of laughter, shades of life
Are ringing through my opened ears
Inciting and inviting me..." Olin Cian murmured, softly singing...

OLIN CIAN ROLLED UP the paper quietly and Ringo stepped down, next to his sneakered feet. He cautiously started to follow behind Kalantha, unseen, with an intense fascination, with Ringo stealthily behind him, singing softly in his oddly accented voice, singing the song Kalantha had playing on her phone ear buds that only she could hear...

"Limitless undying love, which
Shines around me like a million suns,
It calls me on and on across the universe...
Jai Guru Deva, om...
Nothing's gonna change my world
Nothing's gonna change my world

Nothing's gonna change my world
Nothing's gonna change my world
Jai Guru Deva
Jai Guru Deva
Jai Guru Deva..."

OLIN FOLLOWED HER *all the way home*... without her knowing, with Ringo tailing behind, giggling.

KALANTHA'S MUSIC STILL rang out within her old, small studio apartment... the song was one of her very favorites, **"Can't Buy Me Love"**~

"Can't buy me love, love
Can't buy me love...
I'll buy you a diamond ring my friend if it makes you feel alright
I'll get you anything my friend if it makes you feel alright
Cos I don't care too much for money, and money can't buy me love
I'll give you all I got to give if you say you'll love me too
I may not have a lot to give but what I got I'll give to you
I don't care too much for money, money can't buy me love
Can't buy me love, everybody tells me so
Can't buy me love, no no no, no
Say you don't need no diamond ring and I'll be satisfied
Tell me that you want the kind of thing that money just can't buy
I don't care too much for money, money can't buy me love
Owww
Can't buy me love, everybody tells me so
Can't buy me love, no no no, no
Say you don't need no diamond ring and I'll be satisfied
Tell me that you want the kind of thing that money just can't buy
I don't care too much for money, money can't buy me love
Can't buy me love, love

Can't buy me love..."

SHE WAS SINGING WITH it, as usual...

KALANTHA'S SMALL STUDIO apartment was rather sparse, white, and extraordinarily clean, with pretty sheer vintage scarves draped all over the place and over her old vintage lamps. She picked up the scarves from thrift shops and street fairs for a dollar or three for...

She lived right across the street from the Ansonia Hotel, or what was the Ansonia Hotel. It was now mostly condo apartments on 73rd off Broadway. She had nabbed a tiny Studio given to individuals and artists who waited for years on lists to be able to move in. She'd been there about six years, didn't need anything else but was deliriously happy, had a nest egg, and saved everything she had.

It was just that something wasn't *right*, a bit *off*, as if something still was *missing* from her life. She volunteered at animal shelters, soup kitchens, helped with after school programs, loved the kids. I guess you could say she was the queen of volunteering, and had a long list of many friends and well-to do philanthropic acquaintances that truly loved her and was invited to many functions, and had no want for dire need at all, just modestly comfortable and yet she hadn't met someone..."special." Not that she wasn't attractive, Shootie knew she was a lot more than she even was aware of and kept asking her to double date with her and her boyfriend, but always being daftly disappointed.

She wasn't a "dater," she didn't like the bar scene or singles parties, or the atmosphere yet was rarely at home. She had met plenty of eligible others, and she wasn't worried on it, and to her, probably better off without anyone so far she thought. It was so peaceful, why break what isn't even broken? It didn't really bother her, that wasn't it.

So, she would just continue on with her studies, her meditations, her volunteering all over the city when she had her time off, besides her obsession with her "studies." It was more than enough for her, this way of life except for that gnawing little feeling, that something was just *missing,* as if she still wasn't helping *enough.*

She was taking a shower after the day's dirty work, and her phone's music was hooked up to a pod speaker in the studio, dimly lit by a battery operated, tiny tea lite candle in a lantern.

A song was starting up again, and she sang with it while in the shower... **Eleanor Rigby**... she was, as many, a Beatle's lover, and had been listening to this Beatles playlist all day, kind of nonstop for a month now. She even mimicked their accents and wasn't bad at all at carrying a tune.

"Ah, look at all the lonely people
Ah, look at all the lonely people
Eleanor Rigby picks up the rice in the church where a wedding has been
Lives in a dream
Waits at the window, wearing the face that she keeps in a jar by the door
Who is it for?
All the lonely people
Where do they all come from ?
All the lonely people
Where do they all belong ?
Father McKenzie writing the words of a sermon that no one will hear
No one comes near.
Look at him working. Darning his socks in the night when there's nobody there
What does he care?
All the lonely people
Where do they all come from?
All the lonely people
Where do they all belong?

Ah, look at all the lonely people
Ah, look at all the lonely people
Eleanor Rigby died in the church and was buried along with her name
Nobody came
Father McKenzie wiping the dirt from his hands as he walks from the
grave
No one was saved
All the lonely people
Where do they all come from?
All the lonely people
Where do they all belong?"

So many lonely people, she mused, so little time to help them all, yet in her own way she was really trying to... wanting to *help them all.* She just had this innate drive to help anyone she could. Maybe she should join the Peace Corps? Go back to school to be a nurse? Would that do it? Was that the missing piece?

Outside, across the street from her apartment windows was the side archway opening to the Ansonia Hotel. The apartment she lived in was three floors up, old, with large, overly wide windows facing the street below.

Leaning against the huge stones of the Ansonia archway outside across the street ...was that gent Olin Cian, with his conspicuous newspaper still up over his face and patient Ringo sitting at his feet. He pulled the top of the paper down slowly, intense eyes now covered with round-rimmed, holographic sunglasses, glinting, glancing upward at Kalantha's open window, then switching the paper back up in front of his face, hiding it, trying way too hard not to be noticeable and recognizable.

An artsy, upscale resident pedestrian couple walked out of the Ansonia entrance, conversing, engrossed in conversation about some new event, not even giving him a second glance. It was still light outside, that magic time of late dusk.

Kalantha exited her well-deserved shower in a long, lavender, silk-satiny type of kimono Japanese robe of 30's vintage styling, found at one of the many inexpensive pop up street fairs of the neighborhood, just like the scarves. It was not worth much but very pretty, and flattering. Her long, golden hair was wet and she was combing it out, patting it to let it dry. She had no plans for the night after the "hot time" turn down. It just wasn't her nature. She turned up the pod speakers to her music a bit and then walked casually over to the window, sitting and leaning on the large sill, peering out the half open curtains and blinds...

Within You, Without You throbbed out of the speakers to her ears...

"We were talking
About the space between us all
And the people
Who hide themselves behind a wall of illusion
Never glimpse the truth
Then it's far too late when they pass away
We were talking
About the love we all could share
When we find it
To try our best to hold it there, with our love, with our love
We could save the world, if they only knew
Try to realize it's all within yourself, no-one else can make you change
And to see you're really only very small
And life flows on within you and without you
We were talking
About the love that's gone so cold
And the people
Who gain the world and lose their soul
They don't know, they can't see
Are you one of them?

When you've seen beyond yourself then you may find peace of mind is
waiting there
And the time will come when you see we're all one
And life flows on within you and without you..."

She listened so silently to the lyrics, which were to her so very simple, yet arcanely deep and meaningful. She wished everyone could feel them the way she did; or maybe *they did,* but didn't even speak of it.

She looked out and then down, at the Ansonia archway with a proposed vagrant man in odd attire with round, psychedelic sunglasses reading a newspaper, accompanied by his dog, then down to her hand, examining it, wincing.

"I know I *wasn't* seeing things. I *know* I wasn't. What does this *all mean?"* She whispered to herself, about her bizarre hand incident. She knew it wasn't a hallucination, but just *WHAT did* happen, she had no idea. Thank the heavens no one had seen it. Even with all her research and reading of esoteric and spiritual texts and affections she couldn't place it or had any idea of what had happened. Nothing she had read up on had been like this incident. Her eyes worked fine, she knew that. She had 20-20 vision even possibly more acute without any glasses even for reading. She wasn't a victim of heatstroke and hadn't taken any meds and was not a user... at all, never into it; She was always naturally high. She moved off of the sill and nervously paced a bit, glaring concertedly at her hand.

The music abruptly changed then to another song, **Nowhere Man...**

"He's a real nowhere man
Sitting in his nowhere land
Making all his nowhere plans for nobody
Doesn't have a point of view

Knows not where he's going to
Isn't he a bit like you and me?
Nowhere man please listen
You don't know what you're missing
Nowhere man, the world is at your command
He's as blind as he can be
Just sees what he wants to see
Nowhere man, can you see me at all?
Nowhere man don't worry
Take your time, don't hurry
Leave it all till somebody else
Lends you a hand
Ah, la, la, la, la..."

KALANTHA STOPPED PACING and bewilderingly stared at her music speakers. That song *wasn't on* the order of this playlist... at all. She walked over and switched it off to another, the next song to come on the list, then silently moved over to her futon bed and sat upon it quietly, in a full lotus posture, to begin a meditation, clasping her hands in a folded mudra, a special position that held energy.

Her legs crossed into the full lotus posture, like a pretzel. She had meditated like this for a while now, even years, all on her own. What she *didn't see...* was the two tiny superhero figurines jumping out of her backpack and climbing upon her bedspread and softly, secretly crawling *into one of her robe pockets...*

KALANTHA'S BREATHS were slow and rhythmic, deep and full. Her eyes were closed, and she felt the buzz of concentration between her eyes pulsate and grow. She felt the strange sensation on her face, and of behind her eyes, as if her self was distancing from her body, or growing smaller, and her arms and legs felt like strange, sitting, warm logs, or cooked noodles but not connected to her SELF, her consciousness, who *she really was,* just part of a body she was loosely connected to.

A strange squishing feeling began, as if she was this cube and it was being compacted into a smaller version within her body. She started to feel her body's breathing, yet was not controlling it, as if it was automatic, in its own rhythm, and felt her stomach and torso muscles contract and release all on their own.

The breaths sent her even deeper into meditation and she felt the warm, tingle of energy start to rise from the bottom of her spine upward, in strange waves, leaving her in some sort of–it was so hard to describe, like a pronounced ecstatic joy of a feeling, a suspended sense of elongated happiness, when you experience something so happy and joyous there are no words to fully describe it.

In front of her, within her closed eyes of vision, she saw a vortex of spiraling, spinning energy, of lights, lovely lights swirling, swirling, twinkling, and she seemed to start to travel within this energy of light vortex, violet and green. Only she was traveling not with her body, but with her *self.* She still vaguely felt her body there, on the bed, but it was just a lump of flesh to her at this point, not getting her from place to place this time, and thinly connected to what was going on about her.

She felt the warm sweat trickle from her body, from her heat, dousing her in wetness even after the shower. There were more transcendent colors within the vortex now, in front of her meditating, closed eyes and they were so bright and brilliant she ... hesitated, worried what might happen if she continued on the meditation.

She had gone deep before, but this experience, she hadn't experienced just yet. There was brilliant gold and sky blue light, so bright, so beautiful...

On her bed, Kalantha's body started to *glow*, with strange, golden sparkles as with her hand in the park, and growing, tingling, warm energy of light slowly was snaking up her spine with it, twirling like a vortex, a spring, that she was seeing and experiencing...

"Tomorrow Never Knows" started playing on her music playlist...

"Turn off your mind relax and float down stream
It is not dying, it is not dying
Lay down all thoughts, surrender to the void,
It is shining, it is shining.
Yet you may see the meaning of within
It is being, it is being
Love is all and love is everyone
It is knowing, it is knowing
And ignorance and hate mourn the dead
It is believing, it is believing
But listen to the colour of your dreams
It is not leaving, it is not leaving
So play the game "Existence" to the end
Of the beginning, of the beginning..."

OUTSIDE ACROSS THE street, Olin Cian and Ringo were still staring upward at Kalantha's window intently, even seriously, as they leaned up against the side stone archway entrance to the Ansonia. They were alone.

Olin sighed, and then smiled warmly.

"Is it time now?" Ringo quietly voiced.

Olin took off his sunglasses and stuffed them inside his doublet jacket, flicked his eyes down to Ringo, then up to the window, smiling.

"Yes, now," he softly responded.

A strange, sparkling golden misty fog, translucent light enveloped them, with saturated purple and green glowing glitter, and then they... ***disappeared***, just as a businessman in a full suit walked out of the archway stone entrance. He saw the newspaper Olin was carrying fall flatly to the floor, as if someone had mistakenly dropped it out of one of the apartments up above. He curiously picked it up, shrugged, looked upward, then matter of factly at the paper, and then shoved the newspaper under his arm claiming it as his own and continued to just walk away...

Kalantha's body was sweaty, rigid, and glowing circles of light seemed to pulse, one by one, from certain centers in her body upward.

First from the seat of her bottom, a bright red light, it burst out and traveled up, then to her lower abdomen and changed color, to a sunny orange, then upward to her stomach area and changed to lemon yellow, upward to her heart with a vibrant green; upward to her throat, a lovely bright neon blue; close, up to between her eyes, a serene indigo, then to her crown, the top of her head, royal violet-purple.

It seemed to look like a vertical rainbow, blending and brightening. The colors all expanded and created a vortex... and we could no longer now see Kalantha; her body had vibrantly turned into one huge rainbow of lights, swirling, and we saw, from the open window, two glowing bluish-green purple specks swirling in and joining the vortex of light like a cyclone merging together.

Another point of light also joined them of the same color, and the three bright sparkling globes spun about within this vortex of light; the room was encompassed by it, and then seemed to no longer exist, for it had turned into just a vortex of tornado energy, and spinning light, and the specks that were traveling within it, the conscious, spirit specks of **Kalantha, Olin Cian and Ringo...**

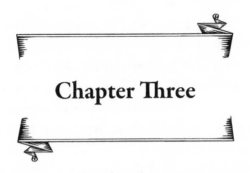

Chapter Three

T he rattle of an old chain and pulley from an old, cruddy elevator clinked and chinked, scraping, as did the "ding-ding!" announcing the arrival, as the floors were being passed. Clearly this mode of transportation was far, far outdated here, yet amazingly still working and holding together.

The 30's styled elevator was descending to the lobby, making its odd creepy noises with it. There was even music playing *in it,* but it was *dub step* music. It was a modern dub-step version of *"Eleanor Rigby"* modern elevator music and it sounded surreal and noir, echoing oddly as that elevator car hit the landing lobby floor of this almost ancient, yet still standing office building, and the door shoddily scraped, then opened wide...

Kalantha was sitting lotus-legged on the floor of that elevator car, seemingly being bumped to alerted consciousness... surprised out of her meditative state. Her eyes popped open and she stared out at the murky lobby in front of the opened, creaky doors. She blinked quickly just to make sure she was seeing right?

Yep, she was.

She quickly sprang up from her sitting position, her reflexes going into panic stealth mode and stuck her head out of the door entrance, staring both ways warily, eyes narrowing, clamping her hands over the doors so they wouldn't close on her, wondering where in the high heaven or hell she honestly *was.*

What on earth was she doing sitting around on the floor of an unknown old elevator? She was just on her bed a few minutes ago. She always took the stairs to her apartment in her old building, it was only three floors up and they were short steps... but this wasn't... *her* old building. It was even OLDER...

"*Hello?* Anyone around?" she ventured to speak, forlornly. "*Oh God...*"

Her voice echoed, eerily, without response. She grasped the elevator doorway and quickly slid out of the elevator, standing her back up against the wall. Then she looked down, at her flimsy clothes. She was still only just in her lavender bathrobe and little slipper flip flops, and... that was *all* she had on, her long hair down and still a bit damp.

Dream. She thought. Was it some dark dream? It was pretty stark and sharply lucid for just a dream. Piles of accumulated garbage and debilitated debris were about the old office building lobby, as if it had been abandoned for years upon years, all dusty and dirty, and the once marbled floor was caked with hard dust.

In front to the right of her there was an old glass revolving door, and *something* was curled up in front of it upon the old marble flooring.

It was Ringo. Ringo stretched, yawned, made a huffy half-sigh noise and then turned towards Kalantha. He stood and slowly meandered over to her, leaving paw marks behind in the dust. Vaguely, Kalantha seemed to remember the little cute mutty pooch. Was he the one from the park ...? Oh, *yes,* he was a tag along with the amazing eyes, and then she had glanced him while looking downward out her window in front of the Ansonia...? How did *he* get *here*? *How did she*? Her mind convoluted, yet on high alert was whirling.

Ringo pattered right on over to her, stood up on his hind legs perfectly and gently placed his front paws upon Kalantha's thighs, wagging his tail and trying to get her trust and attention. He then backed off and walked towards the revolving door, as if gesturing Kalantha to follow him.

Kalantha was very keen on deciphering doggie language, or any other animal communication for that matter. She got the hint, and no matter how freaked out she was, and she was quite freaked out but holding it together, she knew what she should do. Being in a strange dark lobby with only a bathrobe and flip-flops on was enough to do it for her. And this dog was very friendly, well-trained seemingly intelligent and most likely had an owner who could tell her what and where in hell tarnation she was...

Ringo pawed at the revolving door, scratching at it for her to open it. Kalantha obliged, pushed it and it creaked strangely, still abled and working, rotating her out...

The street in front of her was dark, dank, murky, and smelled menacingly awful, like putrid rotting rubbish and smoke, and was lit up every few seconds or so in the sky with what seemed to be... *screaming rockets,* or ...some kind of blue and green *missiles* or *explosions?*

She was in utter disbelief, never even being close to or near such danger. Maybe they were fireworks, but they didn't seem like it at all. They streaked the sky a neon green and lightning blue.

She wished it were fireworks, but not a chance. Some blinking lights zoomed over the street, belonging to what looked like a tiny drone type of hovering mechanical machine, which then scooted off, and up; something you'd most likely see in a Star Wars movie only even more futuristic. It was spherical with reddish lights and Chrystals.

Garbage was everywhere, and everywhere she saw, the buildings were smashed up. Whatever carnage was left of the older buildings around her were half obliterated, smoking and smoldering, as if they were just attacked or hit. Some were still standing, yet most were burnt out and blasted with holes streaked with that neon green and blue. The newer edifices were also bombed, but mostly standing with holes poked in them every few feet, rounded holes that were smoking green.

It seemed to be...no, it couldn't. She couldn't bring herself to believe it but she had to; the remnants of Madison Square Park, New York City, Manhattan. She saw, but could not wanted to deny what looked like the iconic Flatiron building, worn and weary, crumbling but still up. It was one of the only old edifices still standing, and it had on the bottom floor of it... a *Diner?* It had an eatery, with its lights flashing on and off. It was an old fashioned type of a neon-flashing signed Diner blinking "Flat-Iron" on and off.

On the corner opposite the Diner stood a circle of... unkept, disheveled people, seemingly elderly individuals, old and hunched over, gathering around a bonfire burning inside a huge metallic garbage can and gibbering, pettily arguing over something, fighting veraciously with one another for it, trying not to bicker.

They saw and then noticed Kalantha across the street and stared at her for a moment intently, sizing her up, then totally ignored her and continued their hushed unintelligible arguing.

Ringo whined appropriately to gain attention to himself once more, and pawed at something lying on the curb, then snatched it up and turned back to Kalantha, standing up on his hind legs again as if dancing and attempting to hand her what was in his mouth.

Kalantha tried to shake off her trepidation, nervously taking the object from Ringo and staring down upon it in her trembling hands. It was... a paper currency note? It was a money bill with – *Obama?* It had President Obama's face on it, a seven-dollar bill note? It had no mint date on it, at all. A seven dollar note? That really never existed, at least not where she was from, maybe in a gag gift store.

"Oh Shootie, I think you were *right. What have I done?*" she despairingly mumbled to herself, stunned at it all, glaring out at the humming, blinking Diner sign, and the dilapidated, mangled destruction all about her.

Ringo started gently whining again, trotting into the dirty street to cross it, waiting for Kalantha... to *follow* him. He whined again.

Kalantha hurriedly followed, as they both scurried across the curb and towards the Diner doors. Ringo nudged the door open all himself and slipped through, with Kalantha right behind him.

The smell of stale food and stale people hit and wafted in front of Kalantha; the dingy Diner seemed to be packed to the stalls with dirty, disheveled humanity, most of which looked somewhat *old* or *elderly*, or worse for wear. The ones that weren't *old* all seemed to be recuperating from scuffles or sickness. There was a long counter with swivel seats like the 50's, like a soda jerk fountain area.

Those hunched over, mis-matched clothed, elderly looking people slurping soups or gnawing upon what seemed to be bread sticks or hard rolls took up most seats with the counter.

There was a very grand, vintage old as we would know it lighted inspired jukebox in the corner at the end of the counter with someone standing, back turned in front of it, selecting songs to play.

Behind the counter, an old, white haired man with stubble on his cheeks and chin was slowly pouring from a heated glass pitcher some kind of hot drink into a cup with a filthy apron on.

Kalantha bravely took the only available high swivel seat up on the long soda jerk counter, her eyes shifting back and forth quickly, and placed the currency bill in front of her on the checkered counter top. Ringo casually made his way over to the person in front of the jukebox and started pawing insistently at his sneakered foot.

The tune **"Nowhere Man"** started to scratchily play from the Jukebox...

A rare group or gang of younger aged men that looked as if they had just been in a street fight were leaning up against the wall at the end of the counter, and immediately spotted Kalantha who was only a few feet away and what she had placed on the tabletop, and they whispered to each other, nodding. They quickly made their way over to her and practically surrounded her seat, intimidatingly leaning over her, glancing her up and down in a menacing, snide, strange way silently, as if smelling new bait.

Kalantha shifted on her swivel seat, tightening her robe about her, trying not to move and staring over at the old man behind the counter pouring the hot drink to catch his eye on what to do or for some kind of help. He glanced a look at the gang that just surrounded her and quickly backed off, wanting nothing to do with her, shaking.

Kalantha sure as hell felt what the group seemingly wanted from her and they were starting to reach for that money. She didn't want to argue or even stop them, they could have it, just to stay safe if she even could. She only placed it there so she would be able to sit and get some answers, and she got them but they were not positive. She knew she was in a pretty hot spot, knew she now had to get out of it and away from these unfriendly gaggle somehow, but how? The place was totally packed and she had nothing but her damn robe on... why had she followed that little poochie in here? It was after all the dog's money, not hers.

Trembling, she jolted and backed off to stand up off the swivel seat but her back bumped, jostled right into someone. That someone gently took Kalantha's hand and grasped it.

The two-superhero hitchhiking figurines popped their heads out of Kalantha's robe pocket, shaking their heads at the dreaded situation.

"You and *your* bright ideas!" The Wolverine whispered, sarcastically.

"How was I supposed to know where she'd *end up?*" The Luke whined back to him, as they dove back into the pocket.

Kalantha felt that someone take her hand from behind and squeeze it gently, but she couldn't turn around to see them. The dirty young gang members surrounded her on the sides and behind that person who had just took her hand. She did, however, hear a growl below, from Ringo.

"*She's with ME.* Can't you see?" came a soft, authoritative voice from behind her, in some kind of combined cockney English or Gaelic accent.

Kalantha managed to slide off the seat and back up more, into the person holding her hand as the grungy, smelly, beaten-up gang group quickly backed off, wide eyed and frightened.

"*I said she's with ME,* as you can *see-,*" the voice repeated, strongly.

Whispers filled the air, like some domino effect, all about the Diner eerily~

"She's with Olin Cian...

"She's with Olin Cian...

"Olin Cian... OLIN CIAN..."

Absolutely *everyone* in the Diner backed off and *away* from them, cramming into the farthest corner from where they were standing, from this person she couldn't see, Kalantha, and Ringo.

The gent, Olin Cian, started to quickly usher and drag Kalantha out of the diner, as Ringo hopped up and grabbed his money back from the counter, then followed them out, huffing. It was a rather hysterical sight. It looked like some funny comedy slapstick routine, as Olin Cian was moving so fast Kalantha was almost flying, stumbling with those flip-flops she had on, over her feet.They were all now in the middle of the decrepit, darkened street.

Kalantha was warily in resistance mode, scared out of her mind at what was going on and wondering why this stranger had done what he did for her, some kind of abducted rescue.

All of a sudden, a musical song screamingly blared out of nowhere, as if a gargantuan loudspeaker system was set up outside, and everywhere in the debilitated city so that everyone could hear it, as loud and even louder as a war or tornado siren:

"*All the lonely people, All the lonely people, where do they all come from,*
all the lonely people, where do they all belong?"

A line of **Eleanor Rigby** boomed out, all over, followed by a line from
Nowhere Man....

"Nowhere man don't worry
Take your time, don't hurry
Leave it all till somebody else
Lends you a hand
Ah, la, la, la, la..."

Kalantha just froze in her steps, rigid, turning around to face her
enforced rescuer.

"Look you, *Stop*... I said, *stop!* This is crazy! What on earth is going
on here? Besides whatever has happened or is going on, this *music,* and
the *songs,* I know they are all on MY *personal* song list! Where is it
coming from? I know because I was just listening to them before... is
this all real, or am I just dreaming it? I'm trying to wake up, but I'm
not. Is that your dog?" Kalantha defiantly, strongly asked, really quick,
choppy, still stopping dead in her tracks, making Olin Cian spring back
like a rubber band for he refused to let go of her hand.

Ringo questionably and contritely stared up at her, blinking, tilting
his head in that cute doggy way, then nudged Olin insistently to answer
her.

Olin let out a huge sigh, seeming apologetic, getting the cue from
Ringo that he better fess up.

"Yeah, it *is,* and yeah, *they are,* and **yes**, *he is.* I ah, I thought you
liked the songs, though you haven't known me long. What about this
one, better by far?" Olin softly said back to her, nodding, tentative.

The song then playing quickly changed to **NOW & THEN**, a few
bars of it...

"I know it's true, it's all because of you
And if I make it through, it's all because of you
And now and then, if we must start again
Well we were not sure, that I love you..."

"Is that less fretter, your favourite one? It's rarely begun. It makes you feel better?" Cian added.

Kalantha just glared at him incredulously, staring down at his hand so desperately holding on to hers, not having any intention of letting it go.

A few bars of **"I Want to Hold Your hand"** rang out after that...
"Yaah you, got that somethin' I think you'll understand, when I, feel that somethin', I wanna hold your haaand! I wanna hold your hand... "

"Oh, sorry, um, I'm the one who likes that one. Please...I have to hide you. Please. There is danger, I know I'm a stranger," Olin urgently, softly said, pulling Kalantha closer to him.

Kalantha squinted, finally getting a really good look at him and reacted accordingly, tense, recognizing him, a little freaked out.

"You're the newspaper guy... *Ah, aha*, you... it's **you.** YOU were the one hanging out on the street outside my window. *You* were also in the gardens sitting there, *all day* when I... something happened-with my-(she held up her hand) **who are you**? And *your* **dog!** What is *going on*? What the hell has happened, and why are those songs I–

Olin Cian held out his free hand to stop her, to try to calm and quiet her. He smiled warmly, inwardly happy, tickled pink that she had actually noticed him in the garden.

A compilation of the songs that Kalantha had been listening to and playing prior to meeting this gent boomed out all over and all around the decrepit city, different songs in different corners. To her it was surreal. It lasted a few moments and then eerily echoed, then stopped... and was replaced by the warlike sounds and flashing green streaming bombs and lights in the distance, slowly moving closer and closer towards them.

Olin Cian then just seriously, deeply stared at her.

Then he quietly spoke.

"Well now, music, and lyrics, they are very important to your heart, and show things we might not learn without them; it's a start."

Olin, then, looked aside strangely, as if sharing the moment with *someone invisible,* as if staring over to **US** as if "we" were watching them, breaking that third wall and nodded, then looked back over to Kalantha...

"Dear Ringo and I warmly welcome you. The furry chap doesn't really think he's a dog you must forgive him. I hope you do. SO very glad you showed up, finally, yup. He's *my* pup."

"*Ringo?*" Kalantha whispered back to him, peering down at the dog.

Ringo's ears perked up, and he–he made a sound, as if he was...*clearing his throat...*

KALANTHA STARED OVER to where Olin had side-glanced... to *us,* but saw nothing.

They then both had this intensified, mute stare to each other, silent.

"You must have pretty good Karma," Olin then humorously spoke back up, with a slight held-in laugh, briskly starting to haul her again down the street once more with Ringo right next to them just as a strange, hovering high tech riding vehicle came barreling towards them head on, rounding the corner and speeding, as if it had a collision suicide mission course in mind.

The moving vehicle's top hatch opened and an elderly looking human being wearing black, metallic clothing pointed a large, odd weaponry object straight towards them, seeming like a souped up futuristic hand cannon. There were metal plates and wires all attached and sticking out from his skin and clothing, his face and limbs. It looked very uncomfortable to be that way, and even gross, as Kalantha thought when she saw it. The driver aimed the weapon straight to them and shot towards them, laughing maniacally...

Dozens of what seemed to be golf-ball sized spherical orbs shot out of the weapon, encrusted in some form of red, glowing crystals and lights, rather pretty but she didn't think what they were to do matched their description. They made this piercing, whistling sound as they started to barrel straight towards them... Olin reacted quick.

"Those will harm ya... Ok, right. We have to split, lovie. Like I said, you must have pretty good karma." Olin quickly muttered.

"I *do*? How's that?" Kalantha quipped back, mortified...

"Because you ran into ME. I hope we have time for tea," Olin said, with a strange smile.

Olin grabbed Kalantha closely towards him protectively, and peered downward, tapping his high top sneaker next to Ringo on the street floor...

"*Hold on...*"

The street below their feet opened up in a circle right beneath them, and a blue-violet intensified tubed beam of shimmering light encased them all, and they projected in split second time downward, floating through an escape mechanism... *they just disappeared...*

Kalantha and the rest materialized, and she found herself in an underground walkway tunnel, the remnants of a now unused for almost a century or almost more subway tunnel which had been converted, remodeled with slick, circular walls and colorful floor motion lights as you passed or stepped down near them, rather fun to be walking on.

Olin Cian started sprinting, traveling down the tunnel and quickened his pace, still holding Kalantha's hand, taking her with him, with Ringo right behind them. She thought she heard one of them... giggle.

"Look Sir, thanks for the save but this honestly isn't funny, whomever is laughing and from what I just saw *really dangerous!*" Kalantha hotly said, trying to keep up with him.

"*Dangerous...*" Ringo's small, barking voice echoed to her...giggling.

"I know it isn't, it's quite deadly as you factually said. And *someone* saw you *come in, intact,* more than one noticed you I'm sure and they *know you are here.* You need to trust me, Kalantha. *Please,* just trust me, not to fear."

Cian once again looked over to his side as if acknowledging someone invisible, including *"us"* whispering, " Trust me."

Kalantha quickly shot a look down to the dog, Ringo, in utter shock and disbelief... making sure she heard what she did from him, then to where Cian had looked over blankly to once again, not seeing anyone.

"You know my name? How do you-did that *dog* just-

"I know many things about you, many a thing. *So does Ringo.* Like you said, this isn't funny, and now others will know about you too and they'll come after you honey unless I-please stand in front of me, darling," Olin Cian softly told her, urgently.

"*Please stand in front of me darling,*" Ringo urgently echoed.

Kalantha gave him such a look, then an even stranger one to Ringo, in silent shock, doing as told, glancing over her shoulder behind to him in a very worried way. Olin pensively tapped his sneaker again on the floor and they all shot downward within the violet purple blue tube of shimmering light...

Chapter Four

The underground dwelling room chamber was rounded, circular, uncluttered, and overly clean. It had few wants, a high-tech computerlike machine, keyboard console table and panel, a large, very thin, flat view screen taking up half the rounded wall and a thin, periscope tubular object in the middle of the room jutting down from the domed ceiling.

There were a few old, worn wooden sitting stools with a tiny kitchen setup area, an eating table, an all-in one strange, modernized stove, sink, oven/fridge, and no bed. There was just a small, puffy cotton-type memory foam padded rug on the floor, and over it a thin futon type mattress, some old fashioned quilts and cushions on top of that all on the floor, and a large, antique wooden and metal trunk on the side. It was dimly lit with a glowing lantern object also hanging from the ceiling, over the table.

Olin Cian, Kalantha and Ringo materialized within the blue violet light tube, shooting down from the ceiling hatch near the periscope. The hatch quickly closed up above them as they set foot into the room.

Cian finally let go of Kalantha's hand, pulling off his Shakespearian doublet or tuxedo jacket, for it seemed like a concocted mixture of both, with Kalantha still glaring at him weirdly, cautiously, because outwardly it was a very odd dress choice to her, even though it was a stunning piece of attire, fancy, it was, as was *everything else* that was now going on about her a strangely weird frock for him to be wearing.

Cian rolled his long, flowing sleeves up to the elbow from the old renaissance shirt he was wearing, took off the bow tie and cummerbund and hung the jacket on a round stub built into the wall, stopping to look silently over to Kalantha, as Ringo jumped up onto one of the old stools next to the tiny eating table as if waiting to be served.

"What?" Olin proclaimed, as she still glared at him. He knew she was staring at his clothing, and scared stiff, most likely because he was undressing in front of her, albeit it was just the accessories. "I just wanted to dress up, be spiffy for your arrival." A small, sweet smile grinned out from him, and his eyes pleaded an apology. "All right, my humor doesn't cut it, it's rather bad and needs brushing up. Fact is, we all here wear whatever we can find, for survival."

Kalantha continued her piercing look at him, unmoving. Cian sighed guiltily, gesturing to a stool.

"Please, Kalantha, sit down, when you at least *can*. Should I turn on the fan?"

That little dialogue clip was it for her.

Kalantha stood her ground, and then just burst forth, blurting, gesturing dramatically as she went off at him, not able to contain her frustration, but really being as polite as she could be under the odd, tensed situation...so far this Odd individual didn't seem to want to hurt her, but he was indeed just as peculiar as everything else that was going on.

"Survival?" Okay look, forgive my rudeness, and honestly thank you for your help so far with what's happening, and your kindness in all this-whatever *this is, whatever happened to me* but tell me, **where am I?** Do you even know? Tell me where I *am*, what is going on? What is all this? And no funny stuff! I don't know you, but you seem to *know ME,* **and** you're talking in *rhyme,* most of the TIME!" Kalantha's urgent, whispering voice responded, looking about. Then she huffed a

frustrated sigh, for she as well had just done it herself... rhymed her words...

She saw, noticed the tubular mechanism in the middle of the room, and ventured over to the periscope object and peered into it, trying to figure out just what she had barged into. Olin didn't stop her curiosity, in fact he seemed to expect and enjoy it, the expression on his face beaming. He didn't seem to care being bellowed at by her at all.

What she saw in the viewfinder left her trembling. It was a high-resolution image of what was going on outside, up on top, in very high tech remote viewing. The expanse of the war-obliterated city was before her, with a long stretch of twinkling masses, light balls streaming in the dark sky, flying vehicles and diving drones, bombing sounds, and what looked like but she wasn't sure, the NYC harbor way off in the distance where the Ferry once was... yet it all seemed like some futuristic video game, as if someone was only playing a futuristic war video game and she was *inside of it*-but it was actually happening in *real life,* in 3d, to her so hard to believe... for it wasn't a simulation at all.

"This... is absolutely *terrible. Broken,* shining piles of destruction, screaming bombs, as if it's all some hallucinating horrific nightmare... god-awful gruesome! Is that a harbor back further? Are we... near the water? I see some water further, further out. *What is going on? How is anyone, how could anyone be actually living out there?"* Her hardened voice whispered.

Olin Cian crossed over, approaching the desk with the large screen monitor and computer-like machine. He tapped some buttons on the thin modern keyboard. The scene Kalantha was viewing in the periscope was then projected on to the screen seemingly in 3D, along with all the noises outside.

Kalantha turned to look at it, as did Ringo, who whined unhappily. The screen before them showed a large greenish bomb or missile streaming through the darkened sky, obliterating a remaining building or skyscraper, the one that they had just walked by and out of while up on top. It exploded in a fiery flaming mess, with some strange, mushy residue flying around.

Ringo whined sadly again. Kalantha gasped softly, and Olin Cian winced behind her, his eyes just as despaired as hers.

"Forgive me for the rhymes, it comes out in stressful times; I-I can control it. I'll attempt to stop." He sighed. "Well, that one was close. At least I've got you down here now. Dystopian as it can be to your dismay, yes. That shining twinkly terrain you saw was glass. It was rubbish, huge piles of it, the remnants of a skyscraper glass building. *"They"* had a hit on it, just like *"they"* just hit on the other one right now. It's no nightmare, or hallucination as you are thinking, hoping, though seems it. For your question, we are surrounded by water, Kalantha. For your other question of where you are, well..."

Kalantha took in two short breaths, and blew out two long ones, upset.

"I think I already *know* where I am, though I don't *want* to believe it," was her strained answer, still staring hypnotically at the screen, crossing her arms about her defensively, in sensitivity and blighted trauma, very saddened.

Olin Cian watched her a moment, rather curiously, then started talking quickly, keeping his distance.

"Right, ok, you are in a period *after* the war, *almost*. It hasn't ever really stopped; That huge meteor that collided a while back also didn't help things as well. There's not really a government or states anymore, anywhere, as *you* know of it, just bands of gangs, militia, and blokes fighting for what they can get, and a secret underground network of do-gooders when you bump into them; Ahem. It's not a pretty sight as you can see or hear. I've been around, just doing what I can. There's lots of new technology available and much advancement, but *"they"* don't use it the *right way*. Not many do. Right now for them this is just target practice. *"They"* get rather bored and use the tech it as if it's some tantalizing game, but it's not. It never is. Of course it isn't."

Olin Cian leaned a bit towards her, awaiting some kind of answer from her.

"*Meteor?* Is that what did this, and *a-war? What YEAR?* That paper money bill I saw had no mint date and a totally different President on it and it's not in circulation," Kalantha asked, turning slightly to eye him.

She noted this odd individual's appearance again, though he explained his quirky clothes; He was Caucasian, had a fair full head of to die for longish blondish hair under the baseball cap, a bit of light stubble on his face that hadn't been shaved, (not because he didn't want to, seemed like he just didn't have time to or had done it yesterday) she could tell he was very clean and neat in lieu of that, though, even overly clean, unlike all the other people she had seen so far. He would most likely be considered a looker; even jauntily handsome in many eyes in spite of his forced, roughened, worn appearance.

He was young, though. He couldn't be more than his mid or early twenties, and you could tell he hadn't been in the sun for a while for his skin seemed rather pale, and he had these large, hypnotic, even magnetic blue eyes, a strange dark blue; she couldn't remember when she had seen eyes that dark blue, with what might be considered "starry" specs in them.

Maybe, she hadn't-but they were a dark, celestial blue. He was almost six feet tall but just under it she could figure, and a slim, muscularly toned build, alike a dancer or swimmer would have. His voice had an accent, seemed to be English cockney mixed with some sort of Irish brogue but she couldn't place it. He just seemed like an "odd gent of a chap".

He wasn't threatening her, at all, yet she kind of had this feeling... it just radiated out from him that he somehow... *adored her*, but had never even *met* her. He just simply adored her but not in any kind of attracted, physical way. It was **odd. He**-was **odd.** Quirky, like she herself would have been described by others besides Shootie. Shootie, she would just call her a divine space cadet.

Olin Cian ventured to respond politely.

"It's hard to pinpoint the year, I'd say around 2080? 2150? I think most likely a hundred more, give or take a few. This is Manhattan, New York City; Do you see what's left of lady Liberty out there? I don't think you'd want to, being a native New Yorker." Olin Cian again quickly said to her, without any rhyming, finally.

Kalantha once more glared over at the view screen, and she glanced mortifyingly... at a torch-less Statue of Liberty faintly in the distant Harbor. The hand... holding the torch seemed to be blown off, full of green goop. The periscope technology to her was amazing. It could really see that far off from where they were, zero right in, yet it would have been one of the very the last things she'd like to be staring at.

She even actually saw a couple of... *figures, on top* of the statue, inside the antiqued crown head, moving about, seeming to be arguing with each other, one was tall and had a bluish tinge. The other, smaller, rotund and wearing blue too...

Kalantha's eyes hollowed out and she turned tightly to face Olin, mustering some courage to ask even more annoying questions, because she had to; She just had to, no matter what weird response she was most likely going to get from him.

"How did **you**-how did *I-get here*?"

Olin Cian nimbly, quietly crossed over to the kitchen area, taking an old, copper teapot on the stove off and beginning to pour some hot water into three porcelain-type bowls with etched dragons painted on them, making some clunky, nervous, funny sounds as he did it.

"I think you already know **how**, Kalantha. It's just hard to describe, but brilliant of you."

He reached up into a small canister and grabbed some cubes out of it, and dropped them into the bowls, stirring them with some small metal spoons with the ends also shaped as dragon heads. He turned around to stare at her strongly, making eye contact with her.

"You are a *Transporter*. "*They*" had sensed your arrival before it was completed, but so did I, and they haven't fully realized where you *are yet*, which favors us but there's a chance *we could, we might-*

"You're saying *I* transported myself **here?** That I removed myself from where I was just to come HERE? Just I, myself? How? **Why?** Why *here*, why *now*, who are "THEY" that you keep talking about?" She threw back, nervous and agitated.

Olin Cian expected her outburst and quietly crossed back over to her and carefully placed three warm bowls of cupped soup broth on the table in front of them, and placed a spoon in her hand also shaped like a dragon. He pointed his spoon at the computer view screen.

Ringo sniffed his bowl, and then started lapping it up.

"I in truth can't answer the first two, those must be answered by you; number three, "*They*" are the blokes blowing up the buildings, who don't care if anyone or thing is in them. Like I said it's as if it's some recreational, dastardly game to them, never serious. Their minds think it's just fantastic amusement, an unfortunate way to perceive life nowadays. They don't like the music tunes either. Here, do have some soup." He quickly, yet patiently said to her. "I ran out of tea."

Olin Cian pulled over another very old wooden stool and looked over to Kalantha, gesturing towards the seat. Slowly, she watched him and sat, staring down at the spoon and bowl blankly.

Olin continued looking her over, as if fawning over her, smiling. He was glaring at her in a funny, very curious way, trying to contain himself but having a hard time. He even started to strangely chuckle but stopped it out of curtesy.

"I still can't get over that you're finally here, Lovie. You... need something to wear. You don't even have shoes."

"Oh? Finally? And just how long did I *take?* I didn't know I was *expected.*" Was her rather snarky answer; That wasn't all she didn't have, she basically had nothing on under her robe and she was rather unnerved by it; Wouldn't anyone be?

Cian just smiled to her, and said nothing. He then crossed over to the large, old trunk in the corner. He flipped open the heavy latched lid and bent over, rummaging into it. He spoke to her while going thru the contents of the trunk.

"Part of this area of the city here was once the sight of costume rental warehouses. I guess... that answers my clothing choices, right? At least I have artistic creativity. I'm sure something's here for you. Are you eating?"

He stopped to look over his shoulder at her, squinting, as if still in awe she was there.

Kalantha was still just transfixed, staring at the destruction occurring on the screen in front of her, unmoving, rigid.

Cian strode over and turned it off.

"Righto, yes, we can do without this for right now. Not suitable viewing for a meal, teatime or anytime for that matter. We'll eat first."

Cian dragged another stool over and sat upon it, seemingly in a full lotus yoga position very nimbly, gracefully and began to slurp his soup rather humorously.

Kalantha quietly stared at him.

"Come now, you have to eat. There's no way out of it. You are not dead, nor dreaming, if that's crossed your mind. It's neither one, it's just a bit muddled. It shall clear up."

Kalantha made a face, twisting it, and sniffed at the soup. She dipped her spoon in the bowl to taste it, bringing it to her lips.

"Oh, Miso seaweed soup," she softly mustered, knowing the taste and what it was, remarkably.

Ringo made a sound like "Mhm"... and nodded, then continued lapping up his soup.

Cian started cheerfully babbling again.

"Ah, yes, nothing like a good bowl of miso seaweed soup! It helps get all the toxic accumulation out of the bodily system, as does sunflowers to the soil. Everyone tries to acquire and eat it now but not everyone can get a hold of it. It's one of the reasons we are *down here*. It's not safe enough *up there*, not after the green toxic bombs were dropped, and that other weapon vaporized all, ahm, down here there is a ventilator system that screens out all impurities. All the underground dwellings and centers have them. There's an entire network of these-

"I NEED to know how you know of my name and how this *all happened*, Mr. *"Olin Cian."* Who ARE YOU?" Kalantha blurted out to him, injecting fervently, as if a commander in the armed forces. She had had it with the ignoring of her pleas.

Olin Cian sniffed, and coughed nervously. He placed his spoon down and grew quiet. He downcast his very expressive large eyes with a tiny frown.

"He's a *Nowhere Man*. He doesn't belong *nowhere*...with *no one*, *anymore*," Ringo squeaked out, with such a serious tone.

Kalantha just shot an astounded, muted look over to Ringo, then to Cian.

"*Hush, Ringo*. Ok; This is a very personal and sensitive matter to you," Cian softly whispered, chiding his furry friend, blinking, slowly and easing his eyes back to stare at her.

"*Yes,* of course *it is*. Why shouldn't it be? *Look at me. Look at where I am. Look at the talking dog!*" Kalantha with building frustration proclaimed, shakily.

Ringo made a noise like a stifled giggle, then coughed like Cian and continued lapping his soup. Olin cleared his throat.

"Right. Think about *how* you arrived here, what you have been studying for years *on your own*. There are *many* who become this way but not all chose to use their merit and virtue to *aid others*... to show up HERE. *"THEY"* have invented devices, computers, transmissions technology that can sense the materialization of incoming helpful *"Transporters"* like you. Then they home in on you and pinpoint where you are and then they can-they-

Kalantha stood nervously, pointing her spoon at him.

"*Oh,* so YOU used a computer and you-

"No, no lovie; I didn't! I don't have to, with you. I am not with *"them!"* It wasn't needed. I've ... known of you a long time. Quite long-I've loved watching you. YOU did this, not I. You came here out of own free will. I would and could never do that, *take you here,*" Cian told her, alarmed.

Olin Cian reached over towards the computer and pushed some buttons quickly. The view screen clicked back on and the scene of Kalantha materializing inside of the elevator is actually shown, as if there had been a camera pointing down inside at her and filming her. It showed her body frame solidifying, materializing upon the floor of the elevator, and sitting there, with some sparkling mists fading.

"*See?* The memory disc stores all the information, and recorded your arrival, you and others automatically, like a sensor. This is the first time I have seen it. Now that you ARE here, those *"others"* are looking for you *too,* and they'll all want to, um, but I-

A Buzzer alarm rang off, about three times, and interrupted Cian. He flicked at a few keyboard buttons and spoke, softly.

"What is it? This is CIAN. No, I intercepted, she's *here,* with me." He dotingly glanced over to Kalantha warmly. "She's ok, just a bit miffed. I need to explain a few things if I can and then we'll meet at the central."

There was a deep hissing noise that followed, and an ominous deep rumble. Things started shaking a little within the rounded room. The lights dimmed, then went out. Cian quickly turned back on a type of hand held glow lantern hanging from the top of the ceiling from a cord. It swung a bit.

"Section two can you hear me? You can! I just got rattled over here; it may take a little longer. They are going to strike again. Gather everyone for a meeting of the Network members. The *OTHERS* know. Give it twenty; OUT."

Cian deftly snatched a flashlight type object off the wall and swiftly picked up some kind of utility box with parts in it spilling over, and some fell out. He bent to pick them up.

"I'll answer as many questions that I can for you, Kalantha. I need to service something and run some programs. Please, finish the soup, you'll feel better. As soon as I'm done I'll help you with some, uh, clothes."

Olin Cian moved up close to a wall and punched in a code on a small blinking board, then waved his hand over it and opened a large panel built into the wall. He slinked in, bringing the light with him and disappeared from Kalantha's view. There were light tapping noises in the darkness.

Kalantha and Ringo stared over to the open panel. Another rumble was heard and felt within the room, louder than the last, and objects shook and rattled, as well as the stools Kalantha and Ringo were on. Kalantha steadied her bowl and Ringo whined once more.

Olin Cian popped his head out from behind the panel.

"You all right? I felt another hit. You're shaking. Hang on a minute."

Olin Cian crossed over to the trunk, quickly rummaging around and coming up with some costume clothes for Kalantha to wear. He turned and ambled over to her, arms piled high and full. His voice was muddled because of being buried under the clothes.

"These should fit, though kind of opulent. It's the best I could find. Here, they're all yours. You can't walk around in just a robe and flip flop feet, and you haven't finished your soup."

Kalantha just stared up at him trembling, overwhelmed would be more specific, rubbing her eyes as if trying to hide a tear, gritting her teeth and letting it sink in, what was going on about her. Olin dumped the clothes onto the table in front of her and knelt down next to her, gently whispering to her.

"Just like that computer *"they"* have I can home in on you as well, but I have a soul, Kalantha, and I *understand* how you *feel.* "THEY" do not care. They just want to control you, to *use you*; you are something to just pass their time with, cheap thrill amusement abusement. I DO care. I'm a Transporter TOO. And if you don't finish your soup it shall *get cold*, and you *need* to dress. *Let me help you.*"

Kalantha gave him a look, a real strong one, pointing to his bowl.

"It already IS cold and you haven't finished YOURS." She threw back at him.

Olin Cian stood up, swiped up his soup bowl and downed it, placing it back down with a clunk. Kalantha then repeated his performance, taking longer to finish the soup. Ringo used his paw and clunked his bowl as well with a short howl.

"Thank you," Olin shortly sniffed, clearing his throat again and returning back to the panel, disappearing again. Kalantha stood and quickly began sorting through the clothes, examining them, holding up what seemed like a dance costume, a velvet bodice bodysuit and leggings/leotards up to her frame.

"These clothes are just *my size.* Weird." She muttered to herself, surprised. She shook her head and glanced to where Olin was working behind the panel, then slipped on the velvet legging/stockings under her robe, then the velvet leotard bodice on top of them. She took off the robe, now finally covered and threw on a dark blue velvet and ruffled satin shirt, it sort of resembled what a male flamenco dancer would wear, tiered, ruffled sleeves... then pulled up on the funny dark blue velvet elaborate britches, those fancy bottoms resembled something a matador or bullfighter would wear, with a matching vest/jacket, but the britches, they didn't seem to go on right.

"*Oh*, lovie, you have those on backwards. Just take them off and turn them around and they'll slip on and lace up," Olin's voice from behind the panel wafted to Kalantha, just matter of factly.

Kalantha quickly, tensely turned to the sound of his voice, and then stared back down to the britches. There wasn't *any way* he could possibly see her dressing and she fully realized the extent of what he was most possibly doing, or seeing and feeling without his vision with and regarding her, and possibly even more, in mystic perception and eyesight; She shivered and stepped out of the knee-length britches and turned them the right way, stepping into them proper and lacing them up.

The two hiding and silent Superhero figurines quietly scrambled, climbed out of the discarded robe pocket they were hiding from and quickly scaled the velvet vest jacket sleeves Kalantha was placing on. Ringo caught sight of them and started snickering, laughing at them. They waved at Ringo, gesturing for him to shut up and keep quiet. Kalantha stared over at Ringo strangely, having no idea two hitchhikers had climbed into one of the vest pockets she was wearing while adjusting the jacket and pulling on the suede elf like booties. She was looking like a mashup of who knows what from where but it all fit her and she was clothed, but kind of miffed there was no underwear.

There was a power surge and the noise that goes with it, and all the lights and electronics beeped and came back on. Olin Cian stepped out from behind the panel, it sliding shut behind him and made his way back to Kalantha, placing the toolbox and flashlight on the table.

"It's all fixed, at least for a little while. Damage not that extensive. Hmm... your shirt..."

Olin slowly reached over and helped to snap up and fix the open blouse like a mother would. He slowly tied up the frilly bow in front. Kalantha, she didn't pull back from him, just stared at him strangely. He then picked up the dark blue, velvet draped floppy beret, a long hat with a funky tassel on the end, staring at her and grinning in the dim lit room.

"Thanks for the clothes. You couldn't fix the lights...?" Kalantha whispered.

"No, sorry no need for them here, we are leaving. You're welcome." He bluntly told her, soft, placing the hat on her head and stuffing her long hair up into it. "Got to hide this, is shall be spot like gold up there. The cap and coat should help you out, to blend in with the darkness. It's always like that up there. I don't like dark colors they may attract dark and depressive thoughts, but it's safer camouflage. They'll spot you anyway, or home in on you."

Kalantha stuffed more of her hair into the cap, pulling it down over her forehead, listening to him self-consciously, trying to understand what he was attempting to explain to her.

"Remember, you're on the record now, like me. I'm with you, Kalantha; I shall protect you." Cian crossed over to the peg on the wall and grabbed his doublet jacket, pulled it on over his shirt. He stopped short, looking to a long cylinder with a strap on it near Ringo's stool. "These are the Network plans. No time to place it on digital, and too dangerous; No time." He grabbed the waterproof cylinder and slung it over his shoulder. "I'll not leave your side unless absolutely necessary. Please, stand affront me. I'm so glad you're finally here, so very glad."

Cian gave her a quick, soft hug. Ringo jumped down and trotted over to stand with them as a blue violet shaft of light descended, enveloped them and they melted, disappeared within it, and ascended with blurred speed upward as the ceiling opened...

Chapter Five

Kalantha once again found herself materializing within the converted old subway tunnel with Olin Cian and Ringo. It was a tingly feeling, but she felt nothing out of the ordinary as the strange energized tube of light seemed to move them along. Cian started walking quickly, Kalantha's hand in his, Ringo right beside them. The bottom of Kalantha's booties clicked and echoed within the rounded tunnel chamber, while the touch and motion sensitive lights beamed up and about them as they stepped upon them and passed by in the darkness.

"Ah, Mr. Olin? Did you-did you *really get* here the same way I did? Just um, meditating and then-*poof*?" Kalantha brokenly whispered, trying to keep up with him.

"Yes, just showed up here, like you, "poof," only **they** got to me, "*homed*" me first. But I finally broke out of it. I escaped "*them.*" He almost comically responded.

"*Homed*..." Ringo repeated.

"*Escaped? Homed*? I don't know what that means. How *long* ago? How long have you been here?" She pressed him. Olin Cian continued walking warily, glancing over to her as he spoke, hushed.

"A... while. Like I said, "**They**" got me when I first came in, had me 'bout a year or more, I'd say, but not since then. I've been here almost seven years as you think of it. I was just a teen when I came in, on my sixteenth birthday, lovie. I've been through the worst of it. These plans here have helped expand what I've...created."

"And what is *that*, *Mr. Cian*?" Kalantha asked, curiously.

"What you are currently walking in, what you are about to see, what you are a part of now. It's just Olin Cian to you, no need for the Mister or Sir but thanks for being so polite. Can't remember the last time someone addressed me that way, if ever. I'm honored."

"No one properly addresses you? Why not? If **YOU** are the creator of all of this, these underground places? They sure should give you reverence if you *are,*" She unbelievingly asked.

"Yes, I'm the one who thought up and helped create this network... but I'm a very humble creator with a little help, yes, with quite a bit of help from my secret humble followers. I've designed what I could to the best of my abilities in aid of this very bad karmic retribution or bad choice of mistakes of mankind. Yes, I'm the one. Someone cares, yes, someone actually tried to help humankind. Someone was nuts enough to try it. Believe it. It was me. So now you know who I am."

Kalantha gestured towards the cylinder on his shoulder.

"And those are more plans? Are *"they"* aware of all this, what you've created, the ones wanting or trying to destroy everything?"

"Parts of it, not all. They don't know where all of it *is* or the extent of its existence. Technology is pretty x-ray at this point but we have some good buffers and cloaking at times. There is urgent need for construction to survive, but *"they"* make plans too, mainly to destroy whatever little is left, whoever is left. It makes no difference to them.

"I cannot allow that if I have the knowledge to help out. It would be contrary to my nature. At my stage the chi, the energy, the spirit, the vibes whatever you wish to call it, the empathic life force, goes right through me and there are people in those buildings they blow up; people and life forms. They are being killed and I *feel them*, all of them. I hardly expect anyone to get it, to get me, to understand why I did it and are still doing it but that's what I've been up to here and for quite a while. Call me crazy, the *Nowhere Man in charge of nothing.*"

"*Nowhere and nothing,*" Ringo echoed, whining.

Kalantha bewilderingly thought of it, of just what he was doing,
He was honestly trying to, attempting to save the dredges of mankind,
or what was left of it here...it was quite a deep thought to be thinking
while running down a dark tunnel not knowing what was going to be
next for her, but she understood it. She honestly understood why he
wanted to do it, because she would most likely have done the same
thing if she even knew how. She was very much alike he was.

"Olin, I see, and I'm kind of getting it, and the way that energy,
that connection you can feel with everyone and me, *through* me, too?
It's strong, isn't it, that connection you have with me? That's how you
picked up on me? Why you've been tailing me?" Kalantha quietly said.

Olin Cian stopped walking and stared straight at her, stoic. He was
blatantly trying very hard to hold back some upsurged emotions he had
or was feeling, and she picked up on it but said nothing.

"Yes, only with you the connection is stronger and a little different.
Please, hold on again."

Cian ticked his head to Ringo, and he also stood closer to him.

The blue-violet tube of shimmery light encased them once more,
shooting them upward, in the middle of a bombed-out, crumbling
darkened street scene, semi-deserted, with high flying vehicles above,
light balls and fiery blasts in the air. It was just as decrepit and
dangerous as before.

There was an elderly seeming group of people standing in front
of an old building in front of them, squabbling. Olin Cian quickly
started to lead Kalantha towards the building entrance, with Ringo
close behind them. The elderly geriatric group noticed them and
became quiet.

Olin Cian's name was whispered about, and they pointed to a
few boxes at their feet and nodded and they all started to whisper
"thank you," towards him. Olin smiled a tiny small smile and nodded,
entering the building and stepping over some grungy garbage piles and

through the opening, which once held a door, and into a dark lobby with Kalantha and Ringo.

He headed towards an elevator door, waving his hand next to a hidden lighted panel. The elevator door slid open and he quickly ushered Kalantha inside with Ringo, punching some more codes onto another lighted panel inside. The door slid shut and it began to move to another destination, and started to vibrate and hum. They all just stood there very quietly, awkwardly as it moved, until Kalantha spoke up.

"Why has everyone I've seen seem to *know of* you? And most are all so *old*. There are so many *old people*. Why? What was in those boxes they thanked you for?" she questioned, so full of them, of questions, for she really was clueless and felt like she was a freshman in high school all over again.

"Those individuals are not really old; the bombs that had been dropped previously accelerated their aging process, along with the chemical and biological warfare, and the meteor. They just *look* aged. Some are younger than you and I are. I know it's hard to believe but true. Those boxes given to them were food rations and medical supplies."

Kalantha's eyes opened wide.

"Some more of your miso seaweed soup? I guess... that's the reason for your rugged appearance," Kalantha softly said, trying to humor things.

"Oh, that too, nothing like a good bowl of miso seaweed soup," Olin amusedly quipped. "*Me*, rugged? I had no idea." He held back some laughter. He was younger than she was, but as she had noted, had a 'weathered' appearance.

"Why are the people still up ground, up here, if they know it isn't safe why don't they all just stay down where you created a place for them?" she discerned.

Olin Cian sighed, looking out remotely.

"Not everyone thinks the way *we do*; hardly anyone. I'm helping in any way that I can. Their wish is to stay up top. Everyone has his or her own path of life, so many ways to turn and neither right nor wrong. We two just happened to cross the same one, tuned into and traveled on the same wire you might say and so grateful for it. I'm not one to judge, just to help."

As Olin was talking intently, he didn't even notice Kalantha starting to seem to delve in a quiet, trance-like state. He would have but he was in fact babbling. He didn't always feel *everything,* regarding her, especially if he was deep in his own intricate thought.

Kalantha started to grow rigid, and her eyes glassed over.

Olin continued talking, looking straight ahead, still immersed within his musings, and not tuned to her. He was just trying to answer her question in more detail for there was at least some time to do that.

"*Others*, they might call or classify their condition as abnormalities and deformities, but in truth there be no such things. It's just reaction to actions, of body, speech and mind. The *"others"* have warped their perception with cognition twisted from their own obsessive desires. Only they can realize that. We can point the way, but it is all up to them. The Network members help too when possible. We have a few aids, those that help scattered all about. There aren't many of us, but we recruit and do what we can."

"We do what we can," Ringo echoed.

Ringo looked up to Kalantha, noticing her state, for she was now starting to *shake, and mumble...*

"Kalantha... something's wrong with *Kalantha!" He barked out...*

Olin stopped talking and glared over to Kalantha, who was now holding her head and shaking, as if in tremendous pain, unable to speak.

Swirls of what seemed to be grey black smoky light curled out from the elevator sides and began to surround her like a darkened hurricane storm.

She struggled to speak, as Olin attempted to calm and soothe her, very nervously and wracked with blame. He placed his hands upon the sides of her head to steady, to physically heal her with his mystic touch, penetrating her senses and fending off the curling black swirls...

"*Kalantha? No, not her!* Someone must have implanted a *device* in here somewhere to set you up, to *home* you! Try to block the transmission!" he nervously whispered, upset.

From behind the elevator panel a round, red light began to pulsate and glow. Olin took one of his hands and placed it flatly palm down on top the panel in deep concentration. The panel began to warp and melt off and away as if exposed to high heat, exposing a strange, round, crystalized ball that burst into flames.

Kalantha's eyes then popped open, and the figurines stuck their heads out of her pocket, staring up at her, concerned. She started to talk in a strange, monotone voice, as if tranced...

"*Olin Cian,*"*They*" *know of your meeting area, and of your helpers. They will hit here, soon. Sooner than you think so you must depart, all of you. There is one in your group who is of their kind, he was taken, transformed, he is telling them of your plans... you must stop them or he will succeed... and die.*"

"Got to get you out of here," Olin mumbled, grabbing Kalantha's waist and hitting a switch with his foot-

Ringo jumped into Olin's free arm and they all dropped down as the floor to the elevator openly parted, into a blue violet tube of light once more, sliding down and right into a small transport vehicle from the open top hatch, which sealed above them. They all hovered a bit in the cockpit, and then nestled into the two seats, with Ringo in a tiny alcove between them.

The vehicle automatically started shoot forward on the old, converted subway track tunnel as if using the rails as a runway as soon as they were inside.

Olin, still in healing concentration, held Kalantha's face in his hands and stroked her brow, taking deep, slow breaths. There was a swirl of reddish light pulsating about their heads whirling, which then switched to a dark blue, then green, then bright light white gold... and dissolved. Olin's eyes slowly opened and he released his hands from her head, moving back away from her a bit, as to not upset her.

Ringo placed his paw on Kalantha's cheek, rubbing it with gentle concern, along with a whine.

"It's all right Kalantha. I don't think the others found out that much this time, or from you. Your resistance to them is very strong. The *pain*, is it gone? All better?" Cian breathed in relief.

Kalantha straightened up, and opened her shocked eyes to look over to him, a bit out of it and awed.

"*What was that?*" She proclaimed, in disbelief. "How did I-? Whatever it was, it's all gone, all of it. I'm ok. That was horrible! It was as if someone or something was trying to dive into my head and take it over, as if it was a–a cranial *invasion*."

Cian nodded, visibly unnerved and a bit shaken by the incident, and worried that it had happened right in front of him and he didn't even catch on to it, as well as wanting her to be the very last one to be homed.

"Energy and thoughts can be transferred and shared, *yours, and mine*. With us, it is like that. It will always be that way. We are all connected, we all belong to each other but with *us particular* it is very strong. If what you found out is really happening we don't have much time. But we'll handle it. We have to. Thanks for the warning."

"Don't mention it. I think." She dazedly commented.

Two side door hatches flipped up and open as the vehicle came to a stop. Olin quickly stepped out and pulled Kalantha with him, Ringo right at his heels. He moved to the side of the tunnel and waved his hand once again over a panel, then punched some buttons nearby.

Silently a sliding door opened and they entered...stepping right out upon a rounded balcony overlooking from high above, what seemed to be a huge underground dwelling and work area. It could have possibly been Penn Station at one point in time, or Grand Central; Kalantha just wasn't sure but it must have been one or the other, a huge abandoned subway or bus hub.

Men, women, and even a few children were engaged in several tasks. There were garden nurseries to the left, with underground lighting, an area where yoga was being practiced to the right, and some people working on high tech equipment and vehicles behind them. Towards the back more, some domed residential, sleeping and resting tents were set up.

Olin Cian sighed a moment, looking down upon it all quietly.

Kalantha stared over to him, then down at the scene below, rather tensed.

Cian pushed a blue button on the balcony railing and three flute like notes echoed throughout the area. All the figures down below stopped immediately and stared upward towards the balcony.

Cian raised his wrist and spoke into a thin, high tech bracelet he was wearing.

"Everyone, all sections, subsections, please prepare to dissipate to section 2.3; repeat please dissipate to section 2.3 this is Olin Cian. We must leave; GO. Network members to meet now in section 2.7 depart from area immediately. Thank you."

The huge wall behind and below them in the area split in two, sliding open, revealing three large high tech transport vehicles, oval shaped and submersible, pastel lemon yellow in color, like Easter eggs, with intricate designs. Kalantha thought they seemed vaguely familiar, the odd designing of them but couldn't place it in her jumbled mind. All the figures scurried towards them and into them like frightened ants, leaving everything behind.

The huge walls closed up once more, leaving the entire space... deserted.

The superhero figures popped their heads out of Kalantha's pocket to witness the strange spectacle, stared to each other, and shuddering, disappeared back inside.

Kalantha was just stupefied and snuck a frightened look over to Olin, as if he was now some five starred Fleet Admiral in command, which he was, indeed, kind of. He was The Nowhere Man in charge of nothing. Kalantha huddled closer to him, side-eyeing him once more gravely.

"I don't know how I—how I did that, how I said and figured out-

"You are not expected to know; it just comes out in that way. Do you feel anything else? Anything?" Olin warmly responded, reaching out to hold her hand.

"I know, *feel* that particular person will attempt to harm you, and *others* too. I can almost *see* it; he's young. Well, you're young too, but even less than you are," she pensively whispered.

"I shall take you to section 2-7," Olin Cian quickly told her.

Kalantha quickly looked him over, frustrated at the cryptic message sent through her about him, and very worried.

"But I don't see any weapons or anything on you for **defense.**"

"I do not use nor carry them." Olin peacefully said.

"I didn't think you would from what I'm learning about you so far, but you must defend yourself **somehow.**" She pressed, urgently.

Olin squeezed her hand again, his large eyes squinting at her sentence.

"There are ways... to get around such attempts."

Olin Cian turned to open the sliding door back out to the tunnel once more, all of them stepping out.

As soon as they poked their heads forward, a barrage of metal-screaming, blinking lighted balls came streaming down the tunnel flying towards and past them, glowing red, missing them by mere inches. The spheres stopped and hovered in mid-air, as if trying to sense where they were, and strangely the sound of a song as well with them started to echo in the corridor.

"*Help*"...

> "*Help!*
> *Help! I need somebody,*
> *Help! Not just anybody,*
> *Help! You know I need someone, help!*
> *When I was younger, so much younger than today,*
> *I never needed anybody's help in any way.*
> *But now these days are gone, I'm not so self-assured,*
> *Now I find I've changed my mind I've opened up the doors...*"

Olin immediately stood affront Kalantha and Ringo, as some elderly figures rounded the end of the tunnel, spying them, pointing and running towards them with the same cannon-type weapon as before and gross stick-on wire ware, cringing at the music. Ringo started to growl.

"Who and what the hell are *they*? Why are they after **you**? And do you happen to have a digital music system hooked up *everywhere?* **WHY?**" she quickly whispered to him, pressing herself even further towards the wall and behind him, the song blaring.

More of the screaming red balls came flying their way as Olin shielded her and Ringo, pulling Kalantha backward.

"Those unfortunate souls after me are "homed" people. The "*others*" are controlling them. They can't help what they do, and I'm not exactly on their friendship list. They've played me once before and really seemed to like it far too much. I never can seem to shake them. The music? For some reason "*they*" stay away from it, like the plague and I thought you liked it." Olin responded as well as possible within the confusion.

"Help me if you can, I'm feeling down
And I do appreciate you being around.
Help me get my feet back on the ground,
Won't you please, please help me?
And now my life has changed in oh so many ways,
My independence seems to vanish in the haze.
But ev'ry now and then I feel so insecure,
I know that I just need you like I've never done before..."

THEY ALL THEN FELT a huge rumble, and shaking in the tunnel and rattling. The far end of the tunnel started collapsing, caving inward on the group of elderly attackers. Another jolt almost buried Olin, Kalantha and Ringo in crumbling underground infrastructure, trapping their escape and making everything around and above pitch black.

Cian thought fast, and grabbed a flexi- glow tube from inside one of his jeans pockets, where there were many intricate little gizmos to use in a tight spot if needed and snapped, clicked it on, clamped it about Ringo's neck as Ringo started frantically scaling the debris in front of them, his glowing collar now leading the way.

Olin followed behind, pushing Kalantha up with him protectively. They were able to climb over the mass of rubble as best as could and catch a breath.

Olin then closed his eyes and entwined his hands... into a *mudra*, a special hold to pull up energy from within him. It worked for him, this way of things, to build and transmute his energy so he used it, like the kind of mudra Kalantha used when in her meditation. His hands then started to glow bright vibrant neon blue.

He then... placed his fingers upon the side of the wall next to them, tracing an oval about his actual size and width. The wall glowed everywhere he touched it... and *fell outward*, just melting away...

revealing a hole to escape through. Ringo jumped through it and down. The song still eerily echoed in the crumbling chamber...

"Help me if you can I'm feeling down,
And I do appreciate you being round.
Help me get my feet back on the ground,
Won't you please, please help me,
Help me, help me ohhhh..."

"As fast as you can go," Olin whispered to Kalantha, grabbing her with him and down they jumped, starting to book it down the remaining part of the undulating, shaking tunnel that hadn't been destroyed yet, Ringo scampering in front of them.

Olin then stopped abruptly and tapped his sneaker on the ground to find the escape hatch. But... nothing happened. He stared down upon the tunnel floor strangely, disconcerted. He tried it once again, and still... nothing.

Ringo looked up, and stared over and at Kalantha.

She stood very still a moment, then reacted as if she just received some sort of a message, a *silent thought* from Ringo... and she then led Olin back a few paces, pointing down.

Ringo giggled a bit and Olin tilted his head and smiled.

"Brilliant, you found it lovie. I must be tired." He softly whispered, uneasily.

"It's a wonder you *wouldn't be* after what I'm seeing if this is what is normal for you every day; I don't know, I think Ringo, or you... I just knew where it was so don't ask for an explanation." Kalantha mystifyingly said, fast. She was now starting to communicate without even speaking...and wasn't sure she was ready for it.

Cian tapped his sneaker down, and they all disappeared within the blue violet shimmering tube of light once more...

Chapter Six

The shimmery blue violet tube of light beamed all of them down into a rounded, egg-shaped white room, furnished with only swivel white chairs, a long, white, oval table which had a well used, small, portable wooden chess set, open and ready to play, and a high tech computer terminal with a large flat screen built within the table and also hanging on the wall like the one in Olin's dwelling chamber.

Inside of that white the room were fourteen people, humans, network members. They consisted of all ages and races, and wore whatever they could find or still had that was clean, like Cian. They stood pensively, examining the split screen antics, which showed what was happening above ground and in certain underground areas as if the room was a security office center.

The group all turned abruptly as Ringo, Kalantha and Cian came more into focus, solidifying right in front of them. They started to form a tight circle about them as Cian spoke.

"Greetings, and thank you immensely for coming, members. May I introduce... Kalantha to you?"

Kalantha's eyes darted about, quickly accessing and discerning all of the people encircling them. She took a step forward ... and surprisingly stumbled a bit, bumping into a teenager, a younger man who was standing and inching very close to her.

"I'm tripping over my own silly feet. Must be the wrong size boots you gave to me. So dreadfully sorry, please forgive me..." she apologetically whispered as she jostled the teen and stepped back, as he moved away from her.

"Quite all right," the young man responded, clipped, moving back from her quickly.

Kalantha swiftly grabbed Cian's hand rather strongly and stood very close to him, slipping something into his palm and staring boldly over to him, releasing his hand.

Cian stared to her a bit befuddled, for it was to him out of character of her so far to grab *his hand,* he had been the one doing that *to her*- and peered down to his palm. There was a sphere-like object with many crystals jutting out of it lying there, like the ones that had been fired at them previously by the elderly attackers, and the one found within the elevator.

Kalantha started to whisper to him, coughing to cover it up.

"It's him; he was holding this in his pocket," was her strained sentence, through her coughing.

Cian's face dropped, and he continued glaring down at the object, trying to hide it as Ringo started growling. The Superhero figures popped up again, out of Kalantha's pocket to see what was going on and gasped. The Luke figure started to turn on his light saber but The Wolverine stopped him and grabbed him back down to hide into Kalantha's pocket.

"It's a **homer,**" Cian flatly whispered.

All of the Network members noticed and knew what was in Cian's hand and they all started pacing backward in high trepidation. Cian then turned to face the young teenager, Nye, eyes hard.

"Have anything *else* on you? This is a pretty one," Cian grittily asked of him.

"STAY AWAY FROM ME," Nye defensively, darkly growled back to all of them.

Nye bolted across the room, forcibly pushing the Network members aside and away, then abruptly just stopped, and staggered; he dropped faint to the floor like a rag doll, unmoving.

Olin Cian quickly crossed over to him, kneeling down upon the floor and looking him over in observation of his state with Ringo beside him, growling. Olin quickly opened up Nye's shirt, and pulled it up.

Embedded within Nye's stomach and solar plexus was another of those spheres, a *homer*. It had jaggedly stuck itself into him. Cian dropped his shoulders in grief. Kalantha started to move towards them to see what was going on.

"NO, Kalantha, stay back," Olin warned.

Olin Cian touched the back of Nye's neck with his glowing fingers, transferring some of his energy to him.

"He... didn't make it. I'm sorry, Nye. I wish I could have stopped... This room now will be next on their hit. Someone... should stay with him. He hasn't passed just yet to where he should be, he's hanging around, full of guilt and it would help him on the right if someone could point the way. It might be tough for him. I'll do it."

One of the Network members stepped forward, a very old, yet wise and neatly dressed woman with a distinctive voice, and her name was Clorinde. She was one of the real elderly people, honestly very old way past her time and aged naturally.

"No, Cian, YOU are needed to lead. My time is almost gone. There is more to be done and you must complete it with Kalantha. You are not expendable right now. Take the members and Kalantha and your furry "friend" and go. You need to *go*."

Olin stood up and glared at the object in his hands. He closed his fist about it and it crumbled, just crumbled like a fragile toy in his grasp. He shook the debris to the floor and moved over to Clorinde, touching her forehead with his thumb and pointer finger. A glowing, golden light started to surround her, seeming like an energized force field.

"Thank you, Clorinde, for your gracious sacrifice. If it is your choice, so be it. This will help protect you. We have to go." Cian sadly, softly whispered.

He then stepped back and towards one of the rounded sides of the room and touched a button there, waving his hand. A slide door swished open, revealing a platform walkway downward. The Network members all filed past him in a jaunty sprint, into the open walkway and down it. Cian grasped Kalantha's hand and shuffled her to the walkway, turning once more to Clorinde.

"Many more moons to you, Clorinde," he gently said back to her.

"See you on the flip side, Cian. I've been with you since day one, and plainly its time for me too. Don't take too long I have a chess game with your name on it." She sarcastically said back. Cian reacted emotively and nodded, as the slide door swished behind them, leaving her.

Olin quickly walked down the ramp and into a small, oval door with Kalantha and Ringo. The door slid shut behind them with a pneumatic suction sound and whirl. There was a faint tune hovering within the air... Kalantha heard it in the back round... and knew exactly what song it was and gave Olin a funny glance; for it was *Yellow Submarine*...

"In the town where I was born...
Lived a man who sailed to sea...
And he told us of his life
In the land of submarines
So we sailed up to the sun
Till we found a sea of green
And we lived beneath the waves
In our yellow submarine"...

IN FRONT OF THEM IN the dim lighting was a light lemon yellow, distended, oval, egg-shaped interior of an underwater transport vehicle, super high-tech but decorated in resemblance and colors alike a true to life cartoonish "yellow submarine." It was incredible, but so.

There were blinking controls, a long table with swivel seats stuck to the floor and view screens, a blank wall and a closed slide door, and dark rows of what seemed like upright "holders" where the Network members were quickly strapping themselves into and encasing themselves with a clear, see-thru hardened bubble. They were closing their eyes and seeming to quickly delve into some deep sleep or meditation after sliding the bubble structure over themselves.

> *"We all live in a yellow submarine*
> *Yellow submarine, yellow submarine*
> *We all live in a yellow submarine*
> *Yellow submarine, yellow submarine*
> *And our friends are all aboard*
> *Many more of them live next door*
> *And the band begins to play..."*

OLIN LED KALANTHA TO one of the upright "holders" and started to strap her in. She watched his movements, his hands particularly, which seemed to be shaking. Ringo watched him from below.

"Kalantha, if you find out anything else, please tell me, even if you feel you should not," he faintly whispered over to her. "That little trip up of yours was quick thinking and saved everyone. Don't worry on Clorinde or Nye they'll be in a much better place than any of us very soon." He remarked, fixing the straps for her.

Kalantha's face continued her worried gaze on his trembling fingers.

"Well then, there's something, something like a *feeling is* still coming through, it's hard to say it, like a *thought*. Thoughts of wanting to *hurt you*, in an awful way. I can only feel it, but I can't explain *whom* it is, or *what* it is. It's cloaked, or somehow blocked, and it doesn't feel like only one person this time but several." She revealed, as she continued to watch his fingers, which still had a light blue iridescent glow to them upon the tips.

"Right, lovie. I've felt that too, and very close by." He whispered to her, worn out.

Kalantha reached over and steadied his hands, holding them delicately. She could see his physical condition had radically changed, and he was now wearied and fatigued, his energy or his life force had drained, most likely she thought from what she was seeing him do with it and all the glowing produced from it.

She knew and had studied life energy and life force, with all the other myriad of esoteric subjects on her own and that sometimes if you had enough of it and had trained with the utmost precision and the right way, you could transfer your life energy to others and use it for many things, which she saw he was doing and seemed to be some sort an expert master of,-he spoke of it? A Transporter?

She still didn't really have all the answers as to what was going on here at all, but what he was doing with the life energy he had, using it, it was seeming to damage him. She didn't like the looks of that.

"I think you need to rest," She gently pressed.

"I know," he quietly told her.

Olin finished strapping her in and started to strap himself in next to her, yet was having trouble with the last strap; fumbling with it. Kalantha reached over and snapped it for him.

"Thank you," he softly whispered, as Ringo jumped up into the holder with him and snuggled in, starting to ***sing howlingly*** with the song faintly wafting within the submersible.

"We all live in a yellow submarine
Yellow submarine, yellow submarine
we all live in a yellow submarine
Yellow submarine, yellow submarine...."

He squeakily barked out.

Cian reached over and grasped Kalantha's hand, squeezing it, humming with Ringo.

"(Full speed ahead Mr. Boatswain, full speed ahead
Full speed ahead it is, Sergeant.
Cut the cable, drop the cable
Aye, Sir, aye
Captain, captain)"....

"Your energy is flowing and very strong, a healing one. When I touch you we can give or exchange this energy," Cian serenely commented to her, the song continuing in the back round.

"Oh, so *that's* why you're always holding my hand? It figures if we're all going to kick the bucket in this detrimental sour yellow lemon diabolical dunker you're going to take any excuse to do it. I get it now nice set up with the song, it makes it more romantic if you pump the music in *here*, too?" Kalantha humorously kidded, or tried to.

Ringo let out a snorted giggle.

Olin Cian stared over to her with this caught face on, then turned out, looking as if to "*us*" and he burst out laughing. This was a huge rare occurrence for he never laughs. He got it under control quickly though, then glared back over to Kalantha, trying to save face.

"I-I have to transfer as much energy as I can, this... is *important.*"

"As we live a life of ease
Every one of us has all we need
Sky of blue and sea of green
In our yellow submarine..."

"OH YES, IT'S SO IMPORTANT that you have some sort of huge digital stereo system blaring out matching songs to what's going on with us all over the place that you sync up nice, really nice. And you keep doing that, this energy transfer thing, you will not have any more energy left even if it *is* linking with mine," Kalantha quipped.

"It comes back, eventually," he weakly said back to her. "I don't choose *all* the songs that *play*, you know. The system is hooked up to *my thoughts*, and since *your* energy is linked to *mine*, YOU are *also* choosing the songs as well and keeps "***them***" away. Does that *explain the playlist?*" he added, with a comedic grin.

Ringo continued to howl-sing with the song...

> *"We all live in a yellow submarine*
> *Yellow submarine, yellow submarine*
> *We all live in a yellow submarine*
> *Yellow submarine, yellow submarine*
> *We all live in a yellow submarine*
> *Yellow submarine, yellow submarine..."*

Huge power surges were heard. The transport vehicle violently trembled, shaking, and shuddering, bursting into ejection mode. All of the computer and electric lights blinked frantically with the noises and beeps.

"I know there are so many questions, and I'll answer... uh...*oh, no.* **No.** *Bloody hell...*"

Cian winced painfully, and Ringo whined, replicated his "uh oh" sound...

"Olin? Olin?" Kalantha concernedly asked to him, noting the pain he seemed to be in. She squeezed his hand. She then jumped, as the pain he seemed to be experiencing or thinking jolted over and through HER. A light blue-green glowing shaft of pinpointed light from his heart traveled from his chest area over to his shoulder, down his arm and up into Kalantha's hand which was holding his, then through her arm and up, into Kalantha's chest area, her heart, traveling the same route and way, showing the shared energy between them physically.

"Uh-no-mph-*OW-ow*-you're right, this isn't funny. *Oww, ow, can't you stop the transfer of it, the **pain**?*" Kalantha asked him, feeling it *all*...

"Afraid not; when that many souls are hurting I'm going to feel it, and so will **you**. The "**others**" **hit. They** dropped a big one up on top. Manhattan's done for... ***It's gone***, all *gone*. Oh bloody hell, bloody hell ... great. Okay. We just have to continue and keep going," he weakly said sadly.

"Crap," Ringo echoed, sadly.

"GONE?" Kalantha paused, sickened, and distressed. "*Really gone, all of it?*"

Cian nodded.

Kalantha didn't know what to say after that reveal. She was silent a moment, then gathered herself best she could knowing her home was now gone and just shook her head and said the first thing that came to her mind, trying to do what he said to do, just keep going and try to stay calm.

"You actually...*cursed.You curse?* You don't seem the type but sure took you long enough under the circumstances. Where are we ***now?***"

"*Sorry*... we're now in underwater transport. Well, it isn't a usual occurrence for me anymore to be so colourful in tongue, but I do still slang it at times. I usually restrain myself. I at least stopped the rhyming, didn't I?" He sighed greatly. "I'm no angel. If you'd seen the things I've done and I sure don't wish you to, you'd agree. We ... need to move on."

"What about all those people you sent off before? The ones before in that huge gathering space?" she asked, concerned.

"They're out now, and safe."

Kalantha breathed out, relieved. She peered out and over at the other Network members in their holders, encased in their see-thru cocoons, seeming as if in deep slumber.

"The members are in a deep meditative state, at rest and will not wake up until we arrive at section eleven." Olin voiced to her. Kalantha then stared at him, squinty, with a tilt of her head.

"Why aren't *you* doing it? Out of everyone here *you're* the one who needs-

"I *need* to answer your questions and I need to thank you for saving my life and many others. I'm the one who has to give the orders. Looks like we're stabilized now."

Cian unstrapped himself and Ringo hopped out. Cian then carefully unstrapped Kalantha, still shaky and trembling.

"It's okay I can do it myself." She softly told him.

Olin just smiled at her and opened the last strap, helping her out. He gestured behind him, to the table and swivel chairs.

"C'mon, let me show you the plans so you can see them, and the controls."

Olin Cian made his way to the opposite side of the sub, Kalantha following behind him, staring about, intrigued and amazed at how lifelike in comparison the sub was compared to the yellow submarine we all knew of. He pulled a lever upon the wall slowly, and a blue shaft of light beamed down upon the white table and swivel sheets.

He took the cylinder hanging from his shoulder, and disrobed his doublet jacket and cap and hung them over one of the chairs, uncapping the top of the cylinder and sliding the plans out of it and on the table, under a glass plate to keep it from curling up. He also flipped off his high top sneakers and sat on one of the chairs in a full lotus yoga posture, like a trained yogi would. He motioned to Kalantha to come over with a tick of his head, grinning.

"I'm glad you can trust me now, Kalantha. You do trust me, don't you? You wouldn't have followed me here if not." He softly said to her.

Kalantha approached the table with an intrigued silence, standing opposite of him as Ringo hopped into the middle of his lap and settled there, all comfy. She stared down upon the glowing plans, her finger gently tracing over the glass and the blueprints underneath them.

The hijacking superhero figures peeked out of their secret pocket and also looked at the plans, whispering to each other, which Kalantha still blatantly had not picked up on.

The plans were intricate, blueprints for an underground and up top living network; gardens, dwellings, rooms, passages for transport, vehicles, power plants solar, wind and water generated, waterways and treatment centers, some kind of magnetic energy also involved. It was modest but with all necessities and super high tech. It was extensive but masterfully done and put together. An entire city center with off-shoots everywhere.

Kalantha's eyes opened wide, examining it without a sound, then she slowly eased her eyes back across to Olin, in awe of it all.

"This is incredible. I've read up on stuff like this but never really seen...Olin, you are invaluable. You're some kind of futuristic engineer, an architect inventor. I-I can't explain this, If we only had this and used it *now*, I mean, where I had come from. If only they would use and build something like this. Where are we heading? Where is this section eleven? God, why am I asking all these stupid questions you really must think I-

"No, no I don't," Olin injected, with a small smile, eagerly, placing his elbows on the table and staring to her dotingly. "I would never think that. No one is stupid to me. I told you I was here to answer your questions. Quite the contrary, YOU are the one who is invaluable to ME. Fascinating you are to me. Section eleven... is in Ireland."

"Is that where this will be?" She asked him, curiously.

"It's already *there*. It has been for a while. It was only a matter of... well, before the "**others**" found out where we were before. They are not exact on all our locations yet. Study this, Kalantha. If you can, study this carefully and memorize it if possible. It in the future will be something you need to know and build upon. The **"others"** will be after **you** too. They already just tried something on you."

"I'll do my best but I know next to nothing about this kind of... there must be a way to *stop* them. Isn't there a *way*?" She urgently whispered. "There has to be a way, there is so much I think potential with what you can do, or at least attempting to."

"I-shan't strike against them. It's not wise and not my nature." Olin softy replied.

"Something has to be done. We can't just be sitting ducks here on the pond of doom. I know I'm here to help with this, right? That's what I'm here for, right? It sounds ridiculous to me that I am but that's it isn't it?"

"*Pond of doom?*" Ringo echoed, and the superhero figurines mumbled, making quacking noises. Ringo growled to them, a laughing growl, telling them to keep hidden but Olin Cian *noticed them...* he raised an eyebrow but said nothing. Kalantha heard something strange, but was oblivious, overlooked it and didn't question it.

"Well, yes, you've graduated from seedlings to souls, and you are well protected, much more than I. Eventually the effect to their cause will catch up with them. I-have seen that."

Kalantha sighed, shaking her head.

"I can only imagine what else you have seen, being here for so long and creating this entire whatever you want to call it. Please, *who... am I* to you, Olin? Am I just some kind of strange accomplice? Partners in anticrime? You already have a cute furry sidekick what am I supposed to do for you, more daffodil and tulip bulb plantings? *Why you and what for? What ever for?* I – could never be as special as you. I could never create or build such-

"**Yes you can,**" Olin seriously, strongly injected. "*It's not who you are but what WE are. You and I are linked together, your mind with mine; it will grow stronger.* You are just as special, and what we can do **together.**

Think upon all your studies, all the years of it and meditations, your own research with all the religions and esoteric scriptures and dreams.

"*What is it you wanted to do, to desire to create, to BE?* You came here out of your own free will and choice. It could never be any other way. Anything is possible, Kalantha. It's just never permanent but anything is possible. Only your true self is permanent. It changes and grows, that spark within, that *eternal energy,* and it is able to touch everyone and everything, so willing," Cian with intensity professed.

Kalantha eyed him, thinking deeply of what he said of her, and what she now knew of him...

"Then it's possible for YOU to *leave here.* You're a "Transporter" so you say; *you can do that*-you've BEEN doing that *you aren't* trapped here. That's how you were watching me before I came here, right?" She revealingly shot back to him, with a tinge of ire.

"Yes, I can do that," Cian bluntly said, still staring intensely to her.

"Yet you don't even intend to leave here again, right? You just left before because I-

"Right, because it was time *for you* to arrive here, and I was making sure you would be safe. And no, I am not going to leave until what we both have come here for has ended. I am needed here. So are YOU. It's a risk but we can attempt it."

Kalantha glared upon him silently a moment, as if they were having a funky staring contest. She was honestly trying to figure him out.

Slowly she moved around the table, eyeing him. She grabbed off her long, velvet hat and dumped it onto the chair holding his jacket, and slipped off her jacket as well. The superhero figurines quickly clambered out of the jacket pocket and jumped onto her britches, climbing up her leg and into her side bottom pocket, still unnoticed by her.

Kalantha still didn't know what to say or how to react to him, jumbled and full of so many questions but to her they would be useless. She nervously started to pace back and forth, frustrated, misty eyed and emotions fragile. She attempted to ask him more, unsure and uneasily.

"Okay now, I've studied on my own, for many years about many esoteric topics and for so very long I didn't think there would EVER be someone... *ELSE*, at all, working or studying oddly *like* me and for *what* I had no idea and *teaming up* with me, or tailing me. I am not prepared for YOU, for THIS. How long have you known this, how long have you known *of me*? I need to know, let me know. It's not fair that you do and I don't, and following me all around...really, for years? *Years,* like some-some-

"*Pet puppy?*" Ringo butted in.

Kalantha just blinked and meekly stared down at Ringo on Olin's lap. Olin "shhhed" Ringo and picked him up from his lap and stood, placing him back down on the chair. He slowly walked to Kalantha, sitting her down on a seat. He brushed some wetness from her nervous eyes and the tears glowed an iridescent blue on his fingertips as he touched them. He knelt down and held her shoulders gently, staring at her calmly.

"Ok, let me show you. I can at least *show* you. It's all right. We have some time for that. Here now, just sit like I was. You know how you've done it long enough. Let's...take a look..."

Another song started up behind them, on the sub speakers, **The Inner Light,** as Olin helped Kalantha take off her boots to relax and she sat in full lotus posture.

> "*Without going out of my door*
> *I can know all things of earth*
> *Without looking out of my window*
> *I could know the ways of heaven*
> *The farther one travels*
> *The less one knows*
> *The less one really knows*
> *Without going out of your door*

You can know all things on earth
Without looking out of your window
You could know the ways of heaven
The farther one travels
The less one knows
The less one really knows...
Arrive without traveling
See all without looking
Do all without doing..."

OLIN CIAN SAT ON ANOTHER chair facing her, close, and did the same. He placed her hands in a mudra with his left hand, and placed his right hand, his thumb gently on her forehead, and they both closed their eyes. Both of their bodies began to be outlined in a golden mist, swirling about them, entwining gently. The figurines peeked up and out at them wonderingly.

Kalantha's thoughts calmed, and within her meditation with Cian's help, there were visions that she began to see, become one with and a part of visions of who she was, and who he was... *before* they had been Kalantha and Olin Cian. They were short, and they waved, blurred into each other, but she knew it was she, and it was he for she could feel it deep within her being and it made her ache.

She saw two young, dark-skinned young men sitting in front of a guru Indian teacher, listening to a lecture intently. They were poor and in India, many, many years ago; students, together, having no wish nor want but to just be students.

She saw two twin sisters in ancient Japan, arranging flowers in front of an altar of Buddha, praying, in long kimonos.

She saw a young father in 12th century England, holding a baby girl in his arms and crying with joy.

She saw another realm and solar star system, with seemed to be a male and a woman being alike humanoids but more etheric, within a cockpit of a flying space vehicle in space, giving orders to crew members on a space mission.

She saw ancient Tibet, and two male monks studying and copying scriptures and scrolls quietly, in an ancient monastery.

She saw ancient Celtic Ireland, a young man and woman in matrimony attire, running anguished from an angry mob throughout the forest trying to escape, being cornered and about to be murdered.

She saw a gaseous glowing, cloudy, air-like atmosphere, with two playful, luminous light beings entwining and changing shapes, sizes, flying about together and brilliantly melding into each other.

SHE SAW TWO FREE MALE slaves in Pre-emancipated America, transporting and hiding others within the Underground Railroad, acting as spies and liaisons.

She saw World War two, with a young man and a woman meeting at night, shuffling and secretly leading Jews to a hiding place in Germany, then afterwards, being caught and shot to death in a ditch.

She then felt the numbness fade and wear off... and she felt her limbs once more solidly and her body physically connect back to her mind, all warm up and slowly opened her eyes to see Olin gracefully remove his hand from her brow, open his eyes and stare over to her, touching her shoulder slightly, nodding, calm but serious.

She softly gazed over at Olin, studying him carefully, taking in all that she just felt and witnessed without a word for there could be absolutely none to describe it.

Ringo trotted over to them, sat on one of the nearby swivel chairs and watched them, wagging his tail, glaring at the figurines, motioning for them to get back into the hiding place they had. They shook their heads and snuggled back in.

"There are so many, many more," Cian whispered to her curiously. "Those were a just a few chapters. Please rest, Kalantha. It is needed. I must check on a few things."

Cian stood and moved behind Kalantha, softly touching her hair as he passed over to the wall, switching some dials and levers on the blinking panel. "Ireland is not as toxic as most areas. We shall be able to spend "time" up ground, yet even that proposes risks."

He turned to stare back to Kalantha, who was just mutely gazing over to him. He squinted at her, reacting as if she had just said something to him and he crossed his arms defensively, able to pick up her thoughts.

"I *know* you are concerned with my physical condition but do not dwell on it too much. You're still in shock as it is with many questions... *oh, and Clorinde*? She wished to aid Nye cross over to the other side properly. Nye was a bit afraid of the predicament, but he understood he chose it that way. It was highly honorable of her to do that, for she is now with him too. It was her choice and she was right she was about to have her time here up anyway, way overdue; the center we were at is now no more. They are... both now in that in between state, after you are no longer living, where everything is being sorted and they are meeting some of their loved ones and they can soon rest and learn over where they are now.

"Nye is ok too. He knew he chose this plan and he stuck with it, it's taking longer for him for he feels guilty. They both can choose how next to be born when they are ready, to come back. That is up to them. Most do, in our version of what "is". Earth is a pretty good teaching ground. I can see them *both,* and they're smiling at me."

He looked up to his left up about three feet above his head, as if able to see them; there were actually two misted transparent forms hovering there, and then sighed softly.

Olin Cian then peered down at himself, at the dirtied clothes due to the tunnel collapse, feeling uncomfortable. Kalantha didn't get all dusted up as he did. He wiped at them.

"Excuse me, I better change. I shouldn't walk about like this unless I have to. It muddles the energy. I shall be right back."

Cian moved closer to a rounded wall next to the computer panel and pushed it gently, revealing a secret room, disappearing through a hidden slide door with a small, soft "beep" noise.

Kalantha, now alone with Ringo, quickly stood and nervously started walking over towards the sliding door but stopped halfway, turning to the right, opposite the door and next to another rounded wall with a large crack down the center. She faintly heard a number sequence echoing within her mind... as if someone were speaking to her: "22-22-22"—slowly, she approached the small button panel near the crack in that wall and entered the number sequence, then slowly moving back.

The rounded walls started to part and open, folding backwards. It revealed a small cockpit chamber, oval in shape, as if an egg within the egg they were already in with a steering control area; in front of it a large bubbled transparent window, showing the rushing underwater seascape. There were four swivel chairs facing the window with a control board and view screens in front of them, all alight and working in a soft blue-violet light.

Kalantha smirked a bit in awe as she watched the blurry scene in its high velocity in front of her. She couldn't even feel that they were moving that fast, and it filled her with a slight serene wonder. The sound of water running and a muffled shower filled the back round.

Ringo jumped down and tagged along behind her as she turned back around towards the elongated table and its plans, sighing. She crossed over to the door that Olin Cian had vanished behind, standing in front of it, listening to the sound of water spraying and running, placing her hands lightly on the door, tentative. It must have been a tiny shower bathroom.

She felt–she honestly didn't know how she felt at this point but she knew she didn't want to be left *alone*, though grateful for Ringo's company, it comforted her. She also had no intention of joining the tiny shower party.

An echoing, hard CLICK! Was heard behind her, and she spun back around, facing the table with the plans. Ringo started growling, really growling, hard.

Above the table and around the light illuminating it was hovering a moving, contumely mass of grey, a wormlike cloud. Small, threading, curled appendages twirled out of it, spiraling down from the cloud, alike the ones about her in the elevator, touching upon the glass plate which held the blueprint plans beneath it, trying to pry it off and grab them out to try to destroy or kidnap them...Kalantha took a sharp breath in, backing up against the door, never before seeing such an odd, smoky "thing".

The door behind Kalantha shot open and Cian stood directly behind her, his hair damp and shirt almost all back on, he had felt the darkness from the other room and rushed to get himself ready and out there.

He grabbed Kalantha back, removing a silver corded necklace from his neck, which had an opalescent faceted crystal stone hanging from it, dropping it over her head. Kalantha stared down at it, bewildered. Immediately the stone crystal began to glow about her neck.

Olin stuffed his other arm into his sleeve, tied the shirt up quick and protectively stayed put in front of Kalantha. He and she peeking behind him watched silently as the wormy smoky grayish intelligent cloud continued to attempt to pry the glass plate off of the network plans. Ringo menacingly growled once again.

Cian moved a step forward, warily keeping his eyes upon the wormy mass.

"Excuse me but that's MINE," he said, even sounding humorous but it honestly wasn't.

The writhing mass reacted to Cian's words as if it were alive and highly insulted by them, contracting for a moment. Then the smoky tendrils shot out over towards him in split second time, twirling and encompassing him, pulling him down to the floor, dragging him across it and winding about him quickly like thread binding to a spool. Kalantha started to rush over and Ringo barked viciously.

"NO! Stay away!" Cian's muffled voice spoke from under all the wormy tendrils wrapped about him. The Mass had encased Olin like a cocoon, solidifying, as a spider would wind its prey, making him barely visible through the solidifying threads. We heard him softly begin to chant something over and over, some kind of Mantra.

"Ohm- mala mukti- mala mukti ohm Shiva..."

Kalantha started over to him once more, at a loss.

"Stay where you are!" He warned.

The glowing stone hanging from Kalantha's neck began to pulse, as a beam of concentrated red light erupted from it and spread over Olin Cian's encased, imprisoned body form upon the floor. The wormy mass cloud above the table vanished, and gold, twinkling light moved about Cian, still lying there with a coal-like, obsidian structure all over him.

The shaft of red light stopped pulsating and stopped; yet the stone still glowed about Kalantha's neck energetically.

"You...can come over now," Olin's weakened voice sounded, within the encasement.

Kalantha came rushing over, and crouched down over the unmoving, stone-covered body of Olin Cian. She touched the hard, glassy black covering and dug her fingers into it, pounding upon it to try to break through it. Pieces started to crack off, spraying black dust everywhere, and gold sparkles.

Ringo started to paw and dig at it, and the figurines jumped out of hiding and started using their "claws" and light saber to help cut it all off. Kalantha was so engrossed in helping Cian she didn't even see them, as another beam of light erupted from the stone upon Kalantha's neck, filtering over the mass, cracking it. It all started to crumble and break apart, freeing Cian finally.

Kalantha traveled all about him directing the beam from the stone to the areas that hadn't begun to break off. As it crumbled, crystal-like gems also fell out from it, of all different colors. They seemed to look like precious stones; emeralds, rubies, sapphires, diamonds...

Cian sat up, coughing, brushing and cracking the blackened crisp off. Kalantha bent to brush some soot and dust off of him, and Ringo started licking his face. The figurines made this little "cheer" and dived back into Kalantha's pocket.

Cian turned and glared over towards the quietly unmoving meditating members. Kalantha, she watched his expression, which was laden with deep hurt and betrayal. She helped stand him up on his feet firmly, as he sighed sadly.

"Dark thoughts... sometimes you can *see thoughts,* and *turn them* to form. I honestly just showered. What a waste of-

"Are you all right? Are you hurt very badly?" Kalantha whispered. She looked him over but didn't seem to find any abrasions.

Olin just stared down at the floor, seeming embarrassed, looking down at all the soot and gemstones.

"Diamonds and dust. I'm fine, it's just a big mess. Much bigger than I thought; Sorry lovie."

Kalantha stared down to the floor, stooping to pick up a couple of the glittering jewels. They started glowing in her palm. She cradled them carefully and handed them to Cian who accepted them with a small smile.

"A homer didn't do this?" She questioned, confused.

Cian shook his head silently, staring over to her with those star-like eyes.

"Then what *did?* Or, *who?*"

"I told you anything is possible, just not permanent. The *council members...* It could be another homing device, but I don't sense that. They have mentally been *taken control* over, their minds are not their own, and have very strong connections with Nye, all of them. I have taught them best I can but we all have free will. They *didn't* fight it off-they don't think we can make it, make it out, have lost hope of survival so they thought it best just not to fight it. It was the Council members."

Kalantha warily turned to look at the meditating, quiet, council members.

"Can-can the members perceive what just happened? What is going on with them?"

"Not only did they perceive it they CREATED it. All sense the vibrations as well as create them. They are the ones who just *attacked* me. They are the ones who created that *wormy thing*."

Olin placed the gemstones Kalantha handed to him in one of his pockets, and stared down to the stone still glowing about her neck. Ringo licked his hand.

"That stone seems to work very well with you." Kalantha made a motion to remove the necklace but Cian stopped her gently. "No, it's consecrated Hihiirokane, an empowered stone. There's loads of energy flowing thru it from me and the Source. It's *yours* now. I've given it to you and I don't want it back. In truth, if anything happens to me now *you're* next in line to run this thing and *everything else. You know that now, and it is why you are here.*"

"Yup," Ringo quietly spoke.

Kalantha, wide-eyed, glared at Cian and Ringo, bewildered.

"What do you *mean? I just got here!* Olin, *I'm not you*, I-

"You sure are doing a pretty good job for someone who just **got here**," Olin butted in, dusting soot and dirt off his face and body.

Kalantha shook her head and huffed nervously.

"But-but *you are* the one who's-**not me,** I'm just-

"You are the only one who can handle it right now. There is *another,* but he needs a *partner.* His connection is different to me than yours. You'll see and understand. Space and time, are all an illusion as everything else you are stuck in the middle of. You are a Transporter. *Space and time do not have to exist for you. You have mastered them.* You are now able to master many things. It is your choice always, all have that same choice. Is it becoming clearer now?" He forthrightly whispered, in mystic tone.

Kalantha blew out a broken, short breath, shaking her head, flustered, then planting her eyes back on him.

"Well, sort of, yes, *in a way, yes.* I think I understand it. But here? And Now? *I chose this?* I must really be reaching for the brass ring of Dystopia, having a hard time believing my choice. Are any of those council members Transporters?"

Cian shook his head as in no, silently.

"But you said there were ***others,*** like **us**?"

"There ARE," he seriously, deeply answered.

"Then ***where are they all,*** just flitting around?" she humorously spat out.

Cian went to say something, but he sighed, his energy waning, trying to regain his bearing and strength. Kalantha took a hold of his arm to steady him, leading him over to a swivel chair where he sat, full lotus position, staring up at her. Ringo hopped up to sit next to him and he began to pet him.

"Some choose to use it up that way, their ability and energy, not lasting very long if they do; for they then do not resurge the source merit they accumulated and return; I don't deny that, but most are homed when or if they arrive *here,* IF they even wind up, choose *coming here, in this etheric akashic point of time-space;* if they can find it or ask to. A "homer" or being homed is just my simple nickname for it. The "others" call it an "Extirpator."

Kalantha paced back and forth anxiously, soaking his mystic, knowledgeable explanatory words in.

"Okay, I wasn't homed.That's *strange*... Isn't that *strange*?"

Cian shrugged, grateful for her comic flair.

"Like I said, you must have pretty good Karma. They tried, no luck with you."

"What does an Extirpator *do*? A homer?" Kalantha pressed, turning back to stare to him.

Olin bit his lip, seeming very reluctant to answer her, for the first time. His expression changed, as if far off, dazed, and deeply pained. He spoke very softly, staring up to her, forcing an answer.

"*They* can turn you into a walking, working computer droid. You become a DEVICE for their MEANS. Do you remember what it felt like, what was happening to you in the elevator?"

Kalantha moved closer towards him and slowly knelt down near his feet, looking up to him. Ringo placed a paw on Kalantha's thigh muscle reassuringly.

"*Yes,...* I was losing control of my actions, but aware of what was going on about me. It was like... becoming a robot. What... do they *do* with you *after* they home you?"

Olin turned his head away shamefully, not wanting to face her, actually cringing. His answer was emotive, bleak, and dire. Then he turned to look at her with those huge, dark blue starry eyes...

"Oh Kalantha, *anything, anything they want.* They-

Kalantha held out and shook her hand for him to stop. She knew he was about to go into horrific detail but she actually then reached and covered his mouth with her hand and just moved in to hug him tightly. Olin was surprised at her actions.

"I-Kalantha?" he whispered, then placed his arms gently around her, to hug her back, as Ringo made a "aww" whiny sound, moving out of the way.

"*Don't tell me* what they made you do, ok? I'm beginning... to sense it all. And stop thinking it was your fault. It wasn't. I know that's how *you're* seeing it, but it one hundred percent wasn't." Kalantha pulled out of the embrace and wiped more grungy dust off of Olin's clothes, shuddering strangely.

Olin Cian stood awkwardly, trying to gain some composure.

"Ahm-I-I have to change, *again.* I'll be right back," he softly told her, turning back to the showering room, walking to it and in once more, repeating his action.

"I don't care if you're dirty. Of all instances and times to actually...you sure like to stay *clean*," Kalantha called out to him as he walked out of her vision, she knowing he was running away from the intimate moment she had created, and into the other room. The sound of water started running once more.

"Yes, I *do*. It helps clear the energy," his voice sounded, from inside the bathing quarters.

"Will you promise me you'll rest after ? You *need* to do that." She called out.

"I shan't, lovie not enough time for it."

"You seem to have enough time to take a shower, you should be able to slot it in *somehow*. You must, Olin. You have to. I can tell. Whatever you've done so far right now has really used up your energy reserves. You need a recharge."

"My r*eserves?*" He humorously repeated. "I didn't know I was running out of battery juice; And, *I don't sleep.*" Cian then bluntly responded back.

"Well, I **don't either, not the way most do;** you *know what I mean*. I'll watch those monitors, I'll know if there's a problem and I'll know how to fix it. I'm pretty sure of it. Was that *you* telling me how to open the seascape door before? Relating those numbers counting in my head?"

"*Yes,*" He called back softly, just matter of fact.

"Ok, who else would it be? Thanks. They'll be no problem if there is a problem. And *excuse me* if I jolted you with the hug. I guess I'm more of a human being than *you are* at this point." She miffed, laying it on him about it.

Ringo chuckled at that.

"Hugs are nice. I give them all the time," he called back, cheerily.

"You *do*?"

"Sure, *I* just never *get* them."

"Why not?"

"Everyone's *afraid* of me, something... YOU are NOT." He mumblingly replied through the door, honestly.

Surprised at that sentence, Kalantha reacted accordingly. Afraid of ... *him?* That, never even crossed her mind, or heart. He didn't emanate any kind of frightening aura towards her, even at the moment of meeting him. She walked over to the table in front of the seascape window, which had a view screen, headset, and button panel akin to a com-link device.

Music then started wafting thru and from it... getting louder...

"A Little Help From My Friends..."

> *"What would you think if I sang out of tune*
> *Would you stand up and walk out on me?*
> *Lend me your ears and I'll sing you a song*
> *And I'll try not to sing out of key...*
> *Oh, I get by with a little help from my friends*
> *Hmm, I get high with a little help from my friends*
> *Hmm, going to try with a little help from my friends..."*

Kalantha sat down at the table on a swivel seat, in full lotus posture, examining the Network plans within the table as the song continued. Ringo hopped up on a chair next to her. A flash of green light from the com-link board got her attention, blinking on and off. The com-link with some static turned on, then smoothed out.

"Olin Cian? Olin Cian?" A voice from the speaker com-link crackled, and then cleared up.

Kalantha stared down at all the blinky lights and buttons, then reached down, breathed, and intuitively pressed a button; the right one, incredibly.

"Olin Cian is resting. What do you need? *Who is this?*" She asked, curiously wary.

"RESTING? Is this a joke? He never does that. What happened? This is Timothy, Timothy Ban Piobar from section eleven. I am reporting your access code is correct and we have the sub on surveillance mode until destination is complete. Who... is THIS?"

"Who do you *think?*" Ringo chortled.

"*What do I do when my love is away*

Does it worry you to be alone?
How do I feel by the end of the day
Are you sad because you're on your own?
No, I get by with a little help from my friends
Hmm, I get high with a little help from my friends
Hmm, going to try with a little help from my friends..."

"It's Kalantha."

There was a silent beat, as if shock, then more talking from the com-link...

*"**Kalantha?** Hi, Ringo... I knew you'd be there. Kalantha...? Huh... I haven't heard that name in, whoah-wait-**wow**. Cian told me about you about over four years ago when I met him, he said you would come someday and show up... You DID! **HI!** Kalantha, **hi!** He's told me all about-er-uh, what is Olin Cian **doing**?"* The voice mysteriously asked, intrigued.

"I believe he is washing black sooty dirt off of himself. He's in the shower." Kalantha quietly said, rolling her eyes.

"Hmm-sounds like him. He has this thing about black, and dirt, and also, um, well, is he all right?"

"He is exhausted but he is fine."

The song kept on going...

"*Do you need anybody?*

I need somebody to love...

Could it be anybody?

I want somebody to love..."

"*What of the Network members, Kalantha? What is going on there?*" The voice asked, troubled.

"Well, they are all in holders, except for Clorinde and Nye but they... *sigh* something *happened*, something I can't explain or talk of right now, they were thinking of-

"*What has happened? Something is **very wrong** I can **feel it**. I didn't just call here to–Olin Cian wouldn't just-okay, what position did he put you at?*"

"Olin said she was **second in line**..." Ringo barked, as if rubbing it in, giggling, pawing it up to him.

"Uh... yes, he did say that." Kalantha revealed, still very quiet, giving Ringo a weird look.

"**Of his Network?** *Wait a second... I'm... All right look, I trust you, Kalantha, I'm a **Transporter**. **I'd never be anything but honest with you.** I studied under Olin Cian when I first arrived, and stuck with him even after he... I'm in charge of Section Eleven for him and many others. I regard Olin Cian with the utmost respect and dignity. **Please,** push that button on the right, the purple one, twice, then wait a moment, then twice again. Please trust me, Kalantha. You would know if you can't.*" The voice whispered, rather upset and urgent.

Kalantha stared down at the keyboard, hesitating briefly. She glanced at Ringo, who placed his paw on a button, a purple one. The purple one mentioned, nodding to her, tail wagging. Then she did as asked, pressing the button down with Ringo, twice, then again as Tim had asked.

A muffled cushy "THUNK" sound was heard behind them, behind the shower room door. Kalantha and Ringo both turned their heads at the sound.

"Hey, how are ya mate? You-what? *Seven years?* What? *I know,* yeah, she...*showed up.* I know mate. Now get off my toe. Privacy here, geez, **privacy...** I'm taking a shower..." Olin's voice weakly professed behind the door.

The bath door swished open halfway and a tall, mightly muscular man walked out, as the door swished shut behind him. He was a little wet from his arrival point, dressed in a simple yet comfortable cotton linen hoodie pullover, stone grey, short sleeved, with front pockets and drawstring linen pants, matching boots which seemed to come from a time period of long ago, the wrap round style, and some very traditional ancient seeming Celtic/Gaelic scrolling and designed accessories, braided bracelets, a Celtic vest and some half gloves.

His hair was a little on the long side, down to his shoulders, even with a short braid twined near his ear with a piece of grey/gold/blue Celtic decorated thread and linen within it, and charms.

Kalantha noted, and in her mind she kind of even laughed, not aloud of course because she noted his body type matched up like some superhero Marvel/DC Male character, very manly and of the archetype-broad shouldered, biceps bulging, v-shape, face with prominent cheekbones, cleft in the strong chin, chiseled physique, as if he stepped out of a comic book. Interesting that he had time to shave too, just some short stubble. He would have fit in perfectly on that shelf with the other superhero figures in the gardening room that were no longer there...but *here.*

He approached Kalantha at the console com-link table tentative, eyeing her wonderingly and shook his head with a frown, glancing over towards the holders in back, then towards her once more with his strong, almond shaped-glittery eyes.

"Would you believe in a love at first sight?

Yes, I'm certain that it happens all the time...
What do you see when you turn out the light?
I can't tell you, but I know it's mine...
Oh, I get by with a little help from my friends
Hmm, I get high with a little help from my friends
Hmm, going to try with a little help from my friends..."

Timothy continued staring at Kalantha in a weird, shy way. He was nothing but a big-hearted softie, nothing close to "he-man" hulk body builder he resembled. He looked like it, though. He was most possibly in his thirties, maybe even early forties but in fantastic, worked-out shape as Kalantha had described him in her mind; Superhero soldier nature man.

Kalantha couldn't place his nationality or his race. He could be almost anything or a mix of everything; golden skin, wavy medium colored hair the color of light tree bark and eyes a light golden brown, and they glittered, just like gold would. They honestly glittered. It was an interesting combination. She immediately had this feeling and word pop into her mind, of "naturopath" or one very close to nature and working with the elements and energies associated with him. It just emanated from him.

"Do you need anybody?
I just need someone to love...
Could it be anybody?
I want somebody to love...
Oh, I get by with a little help from my friends
Hmm, going to try with a little help from my friends
Oh, I get high with a little help from my friends
Yes, I get by with a little help from my friends
With a little help from my friends..."

Timothy spoke up gently.

"UM, HE'S IN BAD SHAPE. I've never seen him this way. He won't even let me-I'm *very glad* to meet you, Kalantha." Timothy's voice matched his appearance. It was mighty and titanic and everything else. It was just how he said the lines or spoke, his individual empathic softness that didn't match *him.* He stuck out his large hand, and Kalantha clasped it to shake it, her tiny fingers lost in his palm. A pink, auric light with gold sparkles entwined about their shaking hands, and around their wrists and up the elbows as they touched.

Kalantha stared at the energy created by them wonderingly, then up to Tim-he just smiled a big, shy smile, shrugging. He turned and bent down to examine the black, hard chunks on the floor, and the shiny, formed jewels, picking a few up; then giving a wayward, stealthy glance over to the council members in their holders.

He straightened back up and silently sat opposite Kalantha and Ringo in a full lotus position, peering down at the plans. He then slowly eased his eyes back up to Kalantha, making a back thumb movement about the chunks on the floor.

"*THEY* got him pretty good. But that's how he is; always absorbing crap he doesn't have to do, to benefit everyone but himself. And if he keeps it up there isn't going to be anything left *of **him.*** Horrible dirty thoughts touch him, and they turn into these rare, precious shining jewels. That's Olin Cian; Amazing how he can convert dark energy into light that way, elementally."

He placed the jewels in his hoodie pockets, knowing the energy within them would be useful one day for it was Olin's, he would be able to create more Hihiirokane stones with them and give them away to those who could use them properly, and then looked intently at Kalantha with a head tilt, in observation to the opalescent faceted stone hanging about her neck.

"*Hey!* You're wearing his-that ***stone?*** He ***gave*** that to you? Oh lord that means you're really... and he's-" He grew quiet, and serious. "Kalantha, he has been waiting for you for a *very long time.* I don't think you really realize that, or had time to and what you mean *to* him, and he would I think would never reveal it; I believe it is not his nature, being emotive; Time does not exist too much for him anymore. It still does with me. I haven't physically seen him in four years, he just helps me with orders, gives me adjustments and updates every week, tells me to stay put. He's barely aged at all, kind of looks like he's even younger. Weird. He's very exhausted, like you said. You can't really tell, but he needs major rest."

"That's what I told him. I think he listened to me, but he said there's not much time for it, just to take showers," she half-joked.

"Well... that's the first time he's ever listened to *anybody*. He must really... I guess he's known of you a long time. Last time he had been like this was after he was...*homed.* Did he tell you about that?"

"He mentioned it," Kalantha quietly, seriously told him.

"He didn't really tell you what **happened,** did he? He was like that well over a year, **homed.** Everyone got so freaky frightened *of* him and what **he did.** I mean, it *was him, but it wasn't him.* He was like some Jekyll and Hyde, you know, that really old story tale? That's why no one goes near him now. They're too *afraid* of him and the stories about him. Some of it was really, really bad, Kalantha, nasty stuff what they made him *do* and go through, the stories I heard of him were infamous, diabolical, as if he was the worst most wanted criminal known; I wasn't around for that history of him, just right after, but he got through it. I'm very grateful that's all over with. I never expected this to happen, and now. You know, he told me it honestly would, he did. I never thought... why does he have to be right *all the time*?" Tim muttered.

Olin Cian then emerged from the bathing chamber door. He was redressed in a simple sky blue long sleeve hooded linen shirt, and cotton linen drawstring lounge pant to match, half fingerless gloves the same material and tie around boots, attire very closely resembling Timothy's clothes without the Celtic accessories.

"Hey, I made that outfit for you!" Tim warmly exclaimed, proudly, of his tailoring abilities.

"Yes, yes Tim, thank you very much. Thank you, a soul of many talents."

Another song softly started to trickle out in the back round within the submarine...

"Octopus's Garden"...

"I'd like to be under the sea
In an octopus' garden in the shade
He'd let us in, knows where we've been
In his octopus' garden in the shade..."

Olin Cian nimbly walked over to the table and grabbed hold of the plans from under the glass plate holding them down. He placed them back inside the cylinder holder and slung it over Kalantha's shoulder. He entered a code on the button panel upon the wall very quick, crossing over to the alcove with the seascape window scene Kalantha had opened.

He motioned for Tim and Kalantha to follow him with Ringo, and they did, all walking into the area near the seascape window with the shelf table and chairs facing it.

As soon as they came near him and into the area he grasped Kalantha's shoulder tightly, pulling her closer as Tim moved in a bit more with Ringo, a bit concerned and bewildered of why. Cian pulled a large lever upon the wall. The bi-oval walls behind them shut tightly with split second speed and pneumatic air lock. Cian flicked more levers on the side and the tiny seascape sub made a *vvvrooosh* noise, shuddering.

Cian had locked them inside an escape pod sub and it trembled as it was ejected from the mother sub. The large domed window in front of them showed the acceleration of the vehicle.

The song continued in the back round...

"I'd ask my friends to come and see

An octopus' garden with me
I'd like to be under the sea
In an octopus' garden in the shade.
We would be warm below the storm
In our little hideaway beneath the waves
Resting our head on the sea bed
In an octopus' garden near a cave..."

"Hold on right here. It will all level out and be steady in a minute," Cian told them, pointing to a metal bar nearby. Ringo groaned uncomfortably and clamped his mouth on Cian's pants and held on down there. Cian then swiped Ringo up, crossed over towards the large bubble window and sat full lotus position in a swivel seat in front facing it. Ringo hopped into his lap. Cian started typing codes and flicking buttons with lightning speed on the console built into the table. He turned to look over his shoulder at Kalantha and Tim holding on to that metal bar.

The sub stopped trembling.

"We would sing and dance around
Because we know we can't be found
I'd like to be under the sea
In an octopus' garden in the shade..."

KALANTHA LET GO AS she felt the vehicle even out and crossed over to Olin Cian, moving behind him, placing her hands on his shoulders delicately, peering down at him, trying to "humanize him," anxiously awaiting what possibly would happen next. Olin let out a big sigh of dread and sadness, not pulling away from Kalantha's touch.

"Sorry, but that had to be done. The council members will be re-directed to section 8.8-they will be safe, but not of the Network any longer. Can you tell me what you...*feel,* Kalantha? It's important."

Kalantha shifted and winced a bit, then stared out of the seascape window in front of her remotely.

"We would shout and swim about
The coral that lies beneath the waves
(Lies beneath the ocean waves)
Oh what joy for every girl and boy
Knowing they're happy and they're safe
(Happy and they're safe...)"

"WHAT I *feel?* You mean about the council members? Uh-oh-I-I'm sorry." She twitched, as if shocked. "They all want to...I don't want to say it. They, the council members have broken their meditation states and are trying to reprogram the ship to-to-try to go *after you*. Olin, **can** they?"

"Is this really happening, with the members? WOW, it is..." Timothy ventured to say, in stupefied despair, staring over at Olin and coming closer.

"It will *not* be possible, Kalantha. The old programs are deleted. The ones I re-entered are inaccessible. If they shut down the computer system to wipe it out they will be marooned indefinitely under water without power and any way out. The course heading cannot be altered. Just come, sit next to me."

"We would be so happy you and me
No one there to tell us what to do
I'd like to be under the sea
In an octopus' garden with you..."

Silently, with muted reverence Timothy and Kalantha took seats on either side of Olin Cian. They all sat in a row, staring out into the sea window.

Olin turned to take a look behind his shoulder, as if to stare at *"us,"*,acknowledging *"our"* presence with them all, then turned back about. Timothy and Kalantha turned their heads in unison to try to see and decipher what he was looking at behind them, then turned to stare at each other and shrugged their shoulders, at a loss and confounded. They didn't see anything.

Tim grinned warmly and winked to her, shrugging again, agreeing that he didn't see anything either. The figurines in Kalantha's pocket peeked out... and *waved* at Tim. He *noticed* them... and tried not to laugh and said absolutely nothing to Kalantha about it, for she still had not even seen or noticed them. She just raised her eyebrows at Tim, disconcerted, and they turned back around.

"They'll all go after you again you know, bad news here. Why us? Why always us?" Timothy whispered, leaning over towards Cian.

"Why us?" Ringo echoed.

"I know I know," Olin softly said, staring downward, scratching Ringo behind the ears.

"Then they'll be up top soon making other contacts too! Most likely all homed. This is a mess. A huge humungous mess!" Tim declared, with futility.

"I could not keep them against their will, nor should I do anything else. That was more than enough and wished not even to do that. They will at least be safe if and when they resurface."

"But you taught them *so much.* I hope they can remember that. Aw, crap; We really worked hard on setting up all this, and for *years.*" Tim grumbled, very disappointed.

Olin Cian fiddled with some touch-screen buttons and dials on the computer board, trying to be nonchalant but doing a really bad job, and glanced to Kalantha.

"Thank you *again*, Kalantha. Good to see you, Timothy. It's been a *while.* There's a chance we can change it all back around coming up."

Olin and Timothy started shaking a special soul handshake, a long, funny one.

"I am deeply honored," Tim replied, bowing.

"Oh stop that." Cian pushed an intercom button. "This is Olin Cian. Sub number one will not be arriving. Cancel access code on your side. Sub zero one-one is en route to destination. Access code 0-11-3-22. Timothy is on board."

"It's cleared, I'm with them, just us three." Tim said, leaning into the console.

"*Excuse ME?*" Ringo whined.

"Sorry, Ringo, I meant *four*," Tim corrected, with a small laugh.

"*We read you everyone. Hi Ringo; We eagerly await your arrival. Is everything all right?*" A woman's voice on the com-link spoke out.

"As best as can be, affirmative, just a while longer, thank you, Bye." Olin responded.

Olin Cian switched the intercom off, placing elbows on the rim of the table panel and folding his hands in a mudra. He narrowed his eyes and stared off at the blurry bubble window.

"You know, "*THEY*" will come back, in one way or another, *soon*. Sooner than you think," Olin mumbled to them.

"Yup, to try and do *you* in again." Tim almost growled.

"I think they sure *want* to, but... they aren't going to *try* that." Kalantha commented oddly, butting in.

Timothy looked over to her, puzzled.

"They will want to *home*, extirpate him *first*. Killing him would be to Olin's advantage. Death to Olin would be an asset. He wouldn't have to drag his body all around anymore..." Kalantha shockingly added.

Both Olin and Timothy stared over at her, surprised at her deductive wisdom which was indeed truth, then resumed their conversation as Kalantha engrossed herself with staring out into the moving bubble window seascape panorama.

"Right, you're absolutely brilliant. They all would want to home me. They enjoyed it so much the first time I must be their ultimate favorite, doing all their dirty work. I did much too good a job for the wrong side. What I don't understand... is that they never fully tapped into the abilities they really *could use* within me. I'm eternally grateful for that instance. They used me, yes, but as some *warped criminal, incredulous libertine* and... *murderer.* It wasn't fun and I'm absolutely ashamed of it. My reputation is quite infamously nefarious at this point. But I redeemed myself. At least Ringo isn't judgmental."

"Nope, not at all," Ringo added.

"*They* were emphasizing what you were most *least* likely to do purposely, and they wanted to totally crack and shame and embarrass you. It's what "they" do best. Ah, just forget it; How did you finally get out of it, by the way? You never told me." Tim softly asked, intrigued.

"It... just *fell out.* The Homer came loose. It should have finished me off, but didn't." Olin quietly told him. Inwardly, at the time it was all happening he was praying that it would.

As the two were conversing, Kalantha was fixedly staring out the window, noticing something appearing to take shape out there in the ocean depths, something that seemed to be...out of sorts, and her eyes stayed planted on it.

"Uhm... Olin? You mentioned there has been many karmic or physical abnormalities around and about?" Kalantha voiced, strangely. Olin was staring downward at the console of blinking lights, running his fingers over them, reticent.

"Well, you can call it karma, no such thing really as an abnormality, but the cause to the effect, the evolved mutated differences due to the bombs and chemical weaponry, the meteor, the results of all that has happened." Olin replied, gently.

Timothy glanced over at Kalantha, then caught a glimpse as to what she was talking and implying about out the window, which she was so interested in...

It was a monstrously huge CREATURE, crab-like, octopi-squid, seemed mutated and it was dead ahead of them outside the window and *closing in...*

"Well, whatever you want to call that *mechasquidzilla* THING it's heading straight towards **us**!" Timothy alarmingly blurted. Cian's gaze lifted upward to the large bubble window. Another song started wafting over the escape sub speakers...

"Let It Be..."

> *"When I find myself in times of trouble*
> *Mother Mary comes to me*
> *Speaking words of wisdom, let it be*
> *And in my hour of darkness*
> *She is standing right in front of me*
> *Speaking words of wisdom, let it be*
> *Oh, let it be, let it be, let it be, let it be*
> *Whisper words of wisdom, let it be..."*

"*OH*," Olin Cian quickly responded, seeing the monstrous creature and switching the speed controls to slow down the sub and back it up... Ringo started to howl with the song...

Suckered arm appendages shot forward and outward from the huge creature, grabbing the sub ship in its gigantic claw and a large sucker tentacle slammed onto the bubble window, blocking half the view and sticking there...

> *"And when the broken hearted people*
> *Living in the world agree*
> *There will be an answer, let it be*
> *For though they may be parted*
> *There is still a chance that they will see*
> *There will be an answer, let it be*
> *Oh, let it be, let it be, let it be, let it be*
> *And there will be an answer, let it be*
> *Oh, let it be, let it be, let it be, let it be*
> *Whisper words of wisdom, let it be*

Oh, let it be, let it be, let it be, let it be
Whisper words of wisdom, let it be..."

THE SUB INTERIOR STARTED to rattle, making brittle cracking noises. Cian flicked some more buttons as an enormous EYE came close to the window and glared back at them. You could see It honestly wasn't a *real* eye now, or alive. Timothy was right about the mechanical squidzilla joke. You could see behind and into it and there were moving "elderly others" inside the back of the eye as if in a cockpit controlling it.

"You "looking" for something? Catching an eyeful?" Cian toughly remarked, hard.

"Yeah, YOU," Tim gritted, backing away from the table and window, and grabbing Kalantha up off her chair with him... Olin gave him a helpless look.

"We need to get out of here, FAST," Kalantha apprehensively spoke, letting Tim haul her away.

"I don't think I can stabilize this thing, mates," Cian humorously spoke, entering more codes as the sub violently rattled. "Mechasquidzilla looks hungry."

"You don't think... Oh, it's all just one big flaming joke to you! You already know what's going to-always know what's about to happen!" Tim wavered back to him, holding onto the rails of the sub hard with one hand, and Kalantha protectively with the other. Ringo jumped up and dived into Kalantha's arms...

Scraping, strange scraping and drilling sounds were heard near where Timothy was presently standing. He lickety-split jumped over to the other side of Kalantha, still holding steadfastly on to her.

"What are we going to DO?" Tim asked, frantic.

"We *could all* transport ourselves," Cian quipped.

"*No,* can't do it. Your resistance is down and you don't have the energy right now, nope!" Tim blurted back, in truth.

Kalantha apprehensively glanced about and noticed to her immediate left a half-open compartment with its contents jostled out, revealing underwater scuba type gear and strange suits. She grabbed at it with her free hand not holding Ringo and pulled it out. The figurines in her pocket peeked out and stared at each other in disbelief, ducking back in.

"What about THIS? Can we use this? Take them!" She threw a couple of suits at them both.

Leaks about the sub sprang and started to spread, sprouting about the ship. One squirted Timothy right in the eye.

"Oh, great, how far are we from the coastline? Ugh!"

"Very close," Cian told him. "This sub, though, is going to be crunched."

KALANTHA WATCHED OLIN and Timothy catch their suits as she started to step into hers and pull it up and on, placing Ringo down. The suits seemed like a cross between a wet suit and an astronaut suit, but thin and highly modernized, stretching and shaping into each of their bodies perfectly. They all hurriedly dressed into them, as they could be pulled and slipped over their clothes, seeming to mold to anyone's shape or form, as well as hands.

Olin Cian helped Kalantha snap on a transparent bubble helmet encasing her head. He adjusted the backpack and touched a button on her neck on the suit to turn on the intercom system. Cian placed Ringo in what seemed to be a carry pack pouch built into her suit on her back on top of the other backpacks built in, kind of like a papoose for a baby, and snapping a bubble helmet over Ringo as well.

"Do not concern yourself too much with me, lovie. I can sense it within you, If anything were to happen," Cian mumbled.

"I'll be next in line. Right. Don't talk that way I know what you're saying I *know*," Kalantha muttered back.

"You catch on fast. Stick with Tim, he's a fun guy."

"Right, because I have pretty good Karma, right..." she mumbled back to him.

Cian smiled a small, woeful smile at her, and then turned to Tim to adjust his suit, doing the same with him and his bubble helmet. He finished his own himself and opened a small trap door to the right revealing another small chamber.

"You two go on, I will be right behind you. Be careful, and just let it be... you'll see," Cian told them, referencing the song they were all hearing. Timothy gave him a "You better not be saying what I think you are saying" look.

They all stepped into the chamber as Cian punched a button on the wall and the door behind them sealed, as the other one did, with split second timing and an air lock. Water poured in all around them, filling the chamber and submerging them. A hatch on top opened and all were propelled upward and outwards, into the underwater seascape...

Kalantha with Ringo, Timothy and Olin Cian swam under the sea inside the diving waterproof suits automatically able to convert their air breathing somehow with the packs on their back. They shot away from the sub in the distance, which was being crushed and chomped by the monstrous and elaborately disguised fake "creature" built by the *"others."*

Many glowing, iridescent, seemingly psychedelic jellyfish and schools of diverse unique fish swam around them. The sea had a strange, shimmery effect with the various bright luminous creatures. Kalantha thought it might be due to the darkened skies, and the animals in the sea must have evolved more luminescence to help them survive.

Cian propelled himself towards Kalantha with Ringo, and Tim towards her right with the expulsion backpack that worked underwater as well as above, a marvel of an invention as the suits. He dodged a few jellyfish tentacles.

"Everything all right, Kalantha, Ringo, Tim?" he asked of them, on the speaker com-link within their bubble helmets...

"I'm fine, I'm ok," Kalantha responded, with Ringo whining.

"Same here, too," Timothy on his com-link added.

Cian flicked some buttons on the side arm of his suit and he propelled himself to Kalantha's side. He pushed buttons on her arm panel, turning on her backpack. He made sure the cylinder slung on her shoulder was strapped and snapped onto her suit snug.

"Blue button is forward, green is back, white to the left, yellow to the right. Press blue, Kalantha," Olin Cian's voice was heard on the com-link in her bubble helmet and Tim's, as well as Ringo's. Kalantha nodded and pressed the blue button and they both shot forward, as Timothy followed. They were all immersed in a passing school of glowing, oddly shaped "smiling" fish for a moment, and then the school departed. Kalantha kept staring over at Olin Cian, worriedly.

"And when the night is cloudy
There is still a light that shines on me
Shine on until tomorrow, let it be
I wake up to the sound of music
Mother Mary comes to me
Speaking words of wisdom, let it be..."

THE MUSIC EVEN FOLLOWED them into their bubble speaker com-links...

"OLIN, SOMETHING... *something's wrong*," Kalantha whispered, gravely, as Ringo whined again.

"I know you can feel it. I'm *not* going to make it up *with* you..." Olin's voice revealed.

"WHAT?" Timothy blurted.

"Olin...? " Kalantha voiced, trembling.

"*Save yourself* and shoot away from me, NOW." Olin's intensified voice commanded, grabbing Kalantha's arm and punching a code into it.

"Hey! What are you doing? Stop that! NO! NO!" she protested.

Kalantha was thrown and propelled quickly and against her will to the right, and straight into Timothy, just in time and out of the way of a huge, transparent clawed bubble transparent sphere, on top of a fake rubbery squid arm of the mechasquidzilla "creature"... the sphere opened and vacuumed up Olin Cian in one full swoop, hauling him up and away rapidly.

Cian braced himself with the velocity of the rapid upward movement within the mechanism with his arms and feet spread, touching the sides of the bubble. Inside the bubble jetting around was a red, glowing, round homer, crystals and lights jutting out of it and blinking, orbiting around him, trying to find just the right spot... the extirpator whirled dizzily around him. Cian watched it, tried to dodge it yet aware of the futility. He couldn't try to destroy it he was too spent, and the movement of the sphere he was in was too much for him to...

With a deft and fast move, the crystal-encrusted ball dived straight into his solar plexus region, slicing through the underwater suit and implanted itself there. Cian doubled over in the bubble and fell to the floor, clutching the violated, attacked area of his gut.

His entire body began to glow, pulsate a bright blood red...

Kalantha, Ringo and Timothy stared upward at the rapidly moving bubble claw ball, which had captured Olin Cian as they themselves traveled upward towards the right of it, within the sea. It was moving so fast that within just a few seconds they could no longer see it, or Olin Cian...

"*Not again...* he is being HOMED. Oh God, not good! We are *in trouble!* Hook your arm into mine, we'll be ejecting soon." Timothy's voice on the com-link grittily commented, frightened.

"Olin?-no! Tim? Tim, we–we have to-"

"You might as well forget that name for now. He will not be, "Olin" as you *know* him the next time you meet up. *And he will come back. They'll make sure of it.* He'll be someone you'll wish to *forget.* He'll be Mr. Hyde...alter ego... hold on tightly." Tim gravely, sadly told Kalantha, on the com-link.

"*Oh, let it be, let it be, let it be, let it be*
There will be an answer, let it be
Oh, let it be
Won't you let it be, let it be, let it be
Whisper words of wisdom, let it be
Let it be..."

Chapter Seven

Kalantha and Ringo, with Timothy protectively embracing them, broke the surface of the sea and rocketed upward, into the murky sky... their backpacks were also jetpacks, and the high-tech gear blew them right up and out skyward. They were sailing about the dramatic, steep rocky cliffs of the Aryan Islands in high velocity...

It was dusk, the sun almost setting, what you could see or make out of it in the strange, clouded darkened skyline of Dun Duchathair, the ruins of an ancient Celtic rock fort off the coast of Ireland. That, miraculously, was also still standing.

The Jetpacks slowly eased back on their propulsion and Tim with Kalantha and Ringo slowed down, approaching the cliff top ground and gently landed on the surface, still standing up. Timothy let go of Kalantha and she quickly unclasped her bubble helmet and pulled it off, staring outward at the seacoast below her, shockingly upset.

Timothy did the same, unhooking Ringo's top bubble and he jumped out of the papoose pack on Kalantha next to her feet. All of them looked about nervously. It was still daylight out but very misty with clouds above the stunning sunset. They were in desperate mode as they glared all about.

Kalantha...was *feeling things,* things not of her own, of *Olin,* and what was becoming *of* him. The connection and energy of them both had entwined strongly and melted together. She started to try to control her breathing, for the *pain* ... the physical pain and the trauma of whatever was going on with him was too much and she tried to block it...to calm down.

"Olin...*Olin*...you've got to...oh, ***please...***"

Kalantha clutched her arms about her stomach and fell to her knees, gasping and breathing heavily, rapidly, shivering... Timothy attempted to drag her back up in support and Ringo pawed her legs.

"Kalantha? Are you ok? *Kalantha*? There's **nothing** we can do for him right now. There isn't. We have to get up and **go on,** you *have to.* **Please, you can do it, you can,** Olin *needs you* to do it," Timothy strongly told her, holding her up. She contracted again in acute pain.

"*I can feel it,* I can feel **everything** that Olin is going through, his thoughts, his pain*, **I can't stop it. No**...*" Kalantha attempted to straighten back up and take control, to center herself and block the transmission, the connection but she couldn't. Timothy supported her closely.

"It's that telepathic bond... he does that with *me* too. He's done it for years when I was here, it's mostly how I got the instructions to help him out from. It's cool, But not cool NOW when you can feel it as if *he is you.* I know it's really painful, whatever they're doing with him. You're...really connected quite closely to him. I never got that far with him. How um, intimate you two are. You must care for him very much. Can you walk? Can I do something? Uh, *Kalantha...* your *ARM!*"

Ringo whined as they all glared at her right arm, which was glowing a bright bloody red even through the high tech swim/space suit and clothes she was wearing.

She grimaced and zipped down and stepped out of her suit, stripping it off-she undid her velvet satiny ruffled blouse, yanking it down off and exposing the velvet leotard body suit underneath, glancing down at her now bare right arm. From her shoulder to her wrist were big, red, bloody glowing letters, welting, forming a sentence. They were starting to *bleed*... Timothy and Ringo sucked their breaths in, staring down at it in stunned silence.

It read:

HE IS OURS NOW, YOU WILL FOLLOW... sincerely, the BM...

"THE **BM**? Who or what the hell is that?" Tim shakily said.

"You mean *you* of all people don't know *either*?" Kalantha managed to grit out through the atrocious pain...

Timothy just quickly shook his head, mute.

Ringo howled horrendously as if in agony...

Kalantha then heard his voice, Cian's voice, echoing in her consciousness...

"Kalantha, so sorry, do not trust what I say to you except in spirit, do not attempt to help me. Protect yourself and all others when I come. They do not have my soul they can never have that. Kalantha, you must go with Timothy and Ringo and warn the Network..."

Kalantha pulled her velvet satin ruffled shirt back up over her bodysuit top and took a deep breath. She grabbed the suit up as well and hitched it back up with the cylinder still attached to it.

"Which way? We need to contact section Eleven," she calmly said through the immense pain, stone hard.

Timothy stared down at her a moment, disconcerted, and amazed she had pulled herself together enough through whatever she was feeling to continue. He was pretty much in awe of that, and of her. Then he slowly pointed his trembling hand out to the left. He nodded, and began to walk, Kalantha and Ringo following him silently. Tim then touched a button on the wrist of his suit.

"Section Eleven? We have arrived. Important! DO NOT admit Olin Cian until further notice. *Extirpation* has occurred. No admittance for Olin Cian until cleared. Over," he nervously whispered, with a big sigh, even a tear.

"Olin Cian has been-(gasp)we-we need affirmation on that," a voice on the com-link stammered.

"IT'S TRUE!" Ringo wailed, jumping up and down.

"Affirmative, clear only Timothy, Ringo and Kalantha until cleared take all necessary precautions." Tim sadly added.

"We have you all on track scope, but no reading on HIM as of YET. Are you all right?" The voice on the com-link replied.

"We could be better, it's … a huge loss. We'll meet up soon. Out." Timothy sighed greatly and turned off his com-link, looking about warily. "Kalantha? Can you sense anything about Olin's location?"

Kalantha quietly stood there a moment, distant, then twitched.

"I-I can, but it's super ugly, Horrible. He's in some kind of room, a medical room and they are working on him, like an operating table. They all look like they are ninety years old like the other ones who were after him. It's some kind of hardware attachments they are placing all over him, like configuring him into a mechanism. It isn't easy he keeps coming out of the holders they put on him but then they take over him again. They are… *tormenting* him, fooling around with him like he said, mockingly. I don't think they have figured out how exactly to control him, or how to delve into him deep enough to do that, not evolved enough or mature in mind so they are just ridiculing him like a child would." She grimaced "They took all his clothes away, the ones you made for him just ripped them off, destroyed them; he's stark naked now, and… they are clothing him in something *else*. It's all black, clingy and it hurts, all over, and burns…they're really fast with doing it too." Kalantha revealed, in the thought mirage she was receiving in her mind about the incident.

"Yeah, I bet they did, I bet they are. Keep going, Kalantha. We've got to keep going no matter what happens or what "THEY" are gonna make him do, you understand? You're *first in line* right now," Tim's hardened voice said, with rueful distaste, about the description of Olin's torment.

Kalantha, the ROCKS, under the grass, you can use it, it's hidden....

Olin Cian's disembodied voice echoed in Kalantha's mind.

Kalantha looked about. In front of her was a big, rocky area jutting out. She slowly, painfully lifted her right arm to point to the rocks.

"Tim *over there!* A transport system!"

Timothy stared oddly at the area, taking out a small scanner from his suit and pointing it towards the rocky area.

"Funny, I never knew of this location, but the scope definitely reads positive."

Ringo made a strange sound, ran off to the rocks and began pawing on and around the grass, exposing a blinking panel behind a square piece of the pawed sod. Timothy and Kalantha came right after, bending down.

Kalantha ran her fingers over the rocks and lifted the sod of grass and soil gently that Ringo had pawed loose, seeing the computer button panel. Kalantha paused for a moment, then punched in a code-

"22-22, once more... Tim, move to the side quickly!"

Kalantha grabbed Tim and pulled him over and away from the rocks. Ringo jumped up into Kalantha's other arm and climbed back into his little pack halfway down on her back, flicking the bubble helmet back up over himself.

The large, flat slab of rock on top of the rubble pile split open down the middle and up rose a platform holding a small, streamlined air vehicle, platinum gold in color, almost mirror-like, still with the decorations of a yellow submarine but souped up. The doors opened automatically. Kalantha quickly pulled her entire suit and bubble helmet back on and closed and Timothy did the same as she grabbed him and hauled him into the vehicle.

"C'mon!" Kalantha threw him in on the right side and she dove in right after him as the door closed up on them, automatically strapping them in. More music began to filter on to their com-links AND inside the vehicle...

Lucy In The Sky With Diamonds...

> *"Picture yourself in a boat on a river*
> *With tangerine trees and marmalade skies*
> *Somebody calls you, you answer quite slowly*
> *A girl with kaleidoscope eyes..."*

Kalantha stared down at all of the vehicle's high tech panels, switches and dials. It also had a view screen and it was all computerized. She calmed herself and waited a moment...she then intuitively flicked a few switches and took hold of one of the steering mechanisms.

The vehicle rose vertically, as if a helicopter would, with some kind of propulsion fired up from underneath and it then shot forward and upward, quickly speeding over the cliffs and land with smooth accuracy, as if it had some kind of magnetized polarity usage.

Timothy was just giving Kalantha a really far-out strange stare, as if afraid of her, taking the other steering mechanism in his hand.

"Readings in here check out all right. Uh, Kalantha, how'd you-

"He told her! Olin Cian TOLD her he's speaking to her!" Ringo whined, apprehensively.

Kalantha continued to steer the vehicle, actually flying it like an ace pilot, staring straight ahead.

"He-*Olin Cian?* Oh NO, *no no* he's been HOMED! How can you trust him?" Timothy worriedly shot to her.

"Tim, he told me Extirpation does NOT change one's **essence,** It only controls your *actions.* He is STILL Olin Cian. He's speaking to me and I can hear him, it's telepathic. He's helping me pilot this thing too. What he says to me that way is of his own heart, compared to what he is doing physically which is not his bidding. This is what he is telling me, I can feel it; it's terrible. It's as if he's on the outside of his body just looking in, just blocked from everything he is doing..."

> *"Cellophane flowers of yellow and green*

Towering over your head
Look for the girl with the sun in her eyes
And she's gone
Lucy in the sky with diamonds
Lucy in the sky with diamonds
Lucy in the sky with diamonds
Ahhhhhh..."

TIMOTHY NERVOUSLY SIGHED.

"You're right, it's just that... when it **happens,** you *change,* and YOU are DIFFERENT. Your actions are EVIL. He's Mr. Hyde now, not Jekyll."

"Olin is not evil," Kalantha steadfastly commented.

"Follow her down to a bridge by a fountain
Where rocking horse people
eat marshmallow pies
Everyone smiles as you drift past the flowers
That grow so incredibly high..."

"OH, BOY... OK; HOW is your ARM? It looks kinda awful. Can I help with that?" Tim asked, with a caring tone but tinged with apprehension.

Kalantha frowned and shrugged. She was blatantly ignoring the strange, welted glowing lettering under the suit which could still be seen like a neon sign.

A beeping noise went off in the cabin, while a sensor panel near Timothy started picking up a form. He pointed to the radar screen, which was blipping.

"Newspaper taxis appear on the shore

Waiting to take you away
Climb in the back with your head in the clouds
And you're gone..."

"*Kalantha*... something's *out there*, OUTSIDE..." Tim whispered, tightly.

A BANGING KNOCK COINCIDED with the drum roll bangs with the song that was playing in the vehicle... it then traveled from the back of the outside of the flying vehicle to the side of Timothy's window pane area...

BOOM ... BOOM ...BOOOM... BOOOOM-

"Lucy in the sky with diamonds
Lucy in the sky with diamonds
Lucy in the sky with diamonds
Ahhhhh..."

The banging got worse, turning into the seven knock-knock code we all know...

"Oh NO.... *no no no* it sounds like someone knocking to get IN," Timothy's constricted, voice trembled with his innate humor.

Another banging sequence was then heard, on Kalantha's side of the vehicle...

"Picture yourself on a train in a station
With plasticine porters with looking glass ties
Suddenly someone is there at the turnstile
The girl with the kaleidoscope eyes..."
"Boom boom boom boooom...."
"Lucy in the sky with diamonds
Lucy in the sky with diamonds

Lucy in the sky with diamonds
Ahhhhhhh..."

A BLACK-GLOVED HAND appeared, and started knocking upon Kalantha's side window on the oustide. Then, a FACE, a maroon masked face with electrodes hideously glaring into the vehicle popped up, laughing.

It *was* Olin Cian, dressed as an extremely villain-like character, almost humorously, darkly, campy comic book style and he had a black top hat on. How it was able to stick there while he was outside the moving flying vehicle they had no idea with all that wind whipping; it must have been connected to the mask, and he even had a cane in one hand and a cape on his shoulders, fanned out as if he had some kind of bat-winged contraption between his arms connected to the suit. The suit was an all-black stretchy type pleather material and he had a backpack to propel him. There was a lighted cigarette or cigar hanging from his mouth.

He winked slyly over to Kalantha while peering into the window at them. Kalantha kept on steering, eyeing him. Cian's voice penetrated the com-link system inside with a strained, cackling laughter... he was indeed a Mr. Hyde... his voice was heard on the com-link even though he was outside the vehicle...

"Hey there, *Are you going **my way?** Looks like it; You all pick up hitchers, don't you?"*

Cian made a superhuman jump from the side of the vehicle to the front, grabbing onto the nose. Timothy jumped back as he saw him and cowered, staring intently at him, unbelieving.

"He's-OH help us we are in for it now! We are DONE FOR. "They" have total control of his powers! He's just sitting there waving at us like some-some lunatic and grinning. *Look at him!* He wouldn't be caught dead in that get up! Not his style at all. He's more a

Shakespearean type. Maybe... the top hat? I can't believe this! What have they *done* to him? I heard stories but I-I-never saw him, saw him when he was like *this*... just telepathic transmutation, like you," Timothy rambled, wide-eyed, as Ringo yelped, then giggled in a panic.

"I think he'd like the top hat too," Ringo added. "The cane is overkill though."

"*Sweetness, lovie, aren't you going to let me in?*" The com-link cackled, with his strange, maniacal laughter, rapping the cane on the vehicle.

"Would you *look at him!* He's... *throwing Kisses* at you! He's acting like he's Don Juan! Kalantha, you have to do something before HE does! He's moving closer!"

Olin "Hyde" made his way closer, towards the front window.

"*Kalantha...*" Timothy trailed...

> "*Lucy in the sky with diamonds*
> *Lucy in the sky with diamonds*
> *Lucy in the sky with diamonds*
> *Ahhhhhhh...*"

"*What's the idea, mates? You don't like me anymore? Not part of the gang of good guys? Kicked me out, eh? That's rude; If you're good to me I'll not have to do a thing but if you're **bad**...*"

Kalantha pulled at the steering mechanism, glaring up at Olin...

"*Hold on...*"

The vehicle actually pulled up fast, corkscrewing, turning circles and even upside down, spiraling and twirling... then leveling out. Outside in front, "Hyde" had disappeared.

"Whew, well that got rid of him!" Tim whispered, immensely relieved.

Cian's face surprisingly dropped upside down in front of their front window, his tongue sticking out and shaking his finger back and forth with his cane...

"*Naughty naughty naughty!*"

Cian placed his caned hand upon the window and it started to glow a blood red, as did his entire body...

"I warned you..." he spoke darkly.

"Lucy in the sky with diamonds
Lucy in the sky with diamonds
Lucy in the sky with diamonds..."

ALL OF THE COMPUTER panels, dials and switches within the vehicle started to blink and fritz, melting... Olin "Hyde" started to make silly childlike faces at them sticking his tongue out at them again, outside the window...

Ringo howled at him.

"We need to eject, Timothy," Kalantha trembled.

"Why us? But good idea, yes..." Timothy replied, grimacing.

The two side doors flew open; Kalantha bailed out the vehicle with Ringo on the right, Timothy out the left. They then shot upward, backpacks propelling the ascension. They met each other within the sky and hovered there.

"I CAN'T SEE HIM! WHERE is he? WHERE? Is he still-? Timothy stammered on com-link.

Olin "Hyde" abruptly appeared, hovering near Timothy, shaking his cane at him.

"Tim-o-thee! Ohh, Tim-Oh-thee...!" Cian's voice cracked thru their com-links...

Tim tried to back himself up in mid-flight...

"Look you Hyde-Cian ***thing,*** I-you see-

"*That was not a very nice thing to do, mate. Quite impolite and rather heartless, after all I've taught you? I will give you a choice, though. You can become like me, or you can* **DIE...**" Olin "Hyde" laughed out, oddly, puffing on the cig in mid-air.

"WHAT kind of choice is THAT?" Timothy rebuked.

Kalantha shot closer to them both with Ringo, in mid-air.

Cian noticed her, then, and flashed a big smile...

"*Luveee, lovie of all lifetimes, I need to get you ALONE.*"

"Get AWAY from him!" Timothy's distraught voice piped from the com-link.

Kalantha, my belt, it has the extirpator attached to it, to me... if it be possible to get close enough to me and I do not harm you do what is necessary to dispose of it, or me... Kalantha do what you have to do I will always be with you...

Kalantha overheard Cian's voice telepathically, echoing. She listened to the message, and then hovered closer to Timothy, glaring over at Olin "Hyde."

"*Oh, do I have cooties? Have you made your choice? Not to say* **I told you so...**"

Olin "Hyde" poked his cane at Timothy, and a red-hot beam shot out of it and blasted the power pack upon his back. The pack started to smoke, damaged. Timothy yelped and he started to spin in circles out of control in the air...

Olin "Hyde" then turned towards Kalantha, who was trying to shoot over to Timothy to stabilize his pack and help him.

"*MY SPIRIT SWEETHEART, How good you've been! You really must love me. How can I ever repay you?*" Olin's voice snidely said over their com-links.

Cian grabbed Kalantha by her waist, startling her; She did not resist him. He pulled her even closer to him as they hovered in mid-air, Ringo growling. He unhooked her helmet, snapped it off and let it drop out of his hand.

As he did this, Kalantha grabbed for the red, glowing Extirpator sticking out of his solar plexus and tugged at it, shocking him. She pushed some of the blinking buttons on it and broke off some of the crystals, tugging forcibly. It shifted out of him half-way as a gasp escaped from him. He stopped his actions and trembled...

"Kalantha, *thank you*. I... am not saved *yet*. My moods, they will alternate; I'm going to black out. *Please be careful*," he weakly whispered, fainting out and going limp within her arms.

Kalantha grabbed at him, then shot over to Timothy, stabilizing his backpack and hooking her arm into Tim's. She then deftly descended downward with the both of them on either side, incredibly guiding them back down upon the cliffs...

Chapter Eight

Kalantha descended carefully with Olin Cian on one side, and Timothy on the other, able to hold them strongly steady due to their jet packs and landed back upon the cliffs, near a crumbling, ancient rock fort structure. It was getting rather dark now, and the sun had set on them.

Kalantha then gently helped a very dizzy Timothy down to the rocky grass, still holding up Cian, hovering a bit. Ringo popped his bubble helmet off with his snout and jumped out of his pack.

"Are you *all right? Am I?* Contact the base. - Olin Cian? *What happened?*" Timothy mumbled, babbling, popping off his helmet, trying to sit up, disconcerted and loopy. "Is Cian... *is he here?* Is he-oh, *my head... my head...*"

"Just rest, just rest a little, take a few minutes you were spinning like a tornado and now your mind is too," She gently told him, finally touching both feet down.

Kalantha dragged Olin Cian over and a bit away from Timothy, lying him down on the rocks and grass, slipping him out of the jetpack he had on.

Ringo cautiously came over to them, sniffing at Cian's limp form. Kalantha knelt down beside him, examining him like a nurse would. She softly moved his head over to one side, removing the mask-like structure over the top portion of his face and nose with the top hat. Wires slipped out of his nostrils and she did it really slowly, wincing at the bruises and bleeding all over his countenance.

She moved back, slipping all out of her suit and backpack, staring over him again. The stone about her neck started to glow once more... forming a beam. She aimed the beam at the clamps holding a metal structure over Cian's upper torso and the clamps tumbled off of him, melting away, loosening the metal plating and sliding it off.

Kneeling closer to him, she examined more of his headgear and pulled some plugs out of his ears, and noticed more plugs or tacks running the full length of his arms and legs. With care she gently un-plugged them all, removing them, and the ones on his knuckles, slipping off the black gloves he had on. His fingers bled a bit and she tried to wipe them clean with some of her blouse shirt.

She then tentatively stared down at the half-embedded Extirpator in Cian's Solar Plexus area, some of the crystals flickering with light. Cian stirred a bit, opening his eyes halfway...hoarsely whispering to her.

"Your *arm*-is Timothy-

"I'm *all right*. Tim's fine, he's just dizzy he'll come through."

Olin attempted to pull himself up and painfully stared up to Kalantha, then down to the Extirpator. His now bloodshot eyes squinted, and he made a sudden jerky move, grabbing Kalantha roughly and pinning her forcibly down under him, lying atop her on the rocky ground. Ringo whined and backed off. Cian then laughed at her, an insane, evil, cackling laugh. Kalantha did not move.

"*You're not afraid of me, are you? What a spitfire! I have a little round present awaiting you, just like mine, and you don't have to worry about making any decisions because we do it all for you! Transporter spirit you are OURS!*" Cian spit out intimidatingly, taking a puff of his cigarette, which miraculously was still in his hand, then blowing the smoke in her face.

He then threw the cig off and started to kiss her, hard. After a brief moment, his eyes popped open... and he mutely glared in shock down at her beneath him, pulling upward, having no idea what he had done.

"Sorry,...sorry," he painfully whispered, glaring down at the Extirpator. "Please, Kalantha, please, just pull it OUT before *"they"* try anything else!"

Kalantha rose up halfway, woefully staring upon him. He began doubling over in dreadful pain.

"If I do that... I might lose you," she quietly said, so serious, and concerned, so very intensely afraid.

"You will NEVER lose me," he forcefully said back to her.

Kalantha moved out from under him to Olin's side, her emotions torn. Then with a short, hard breath, and with one deft and forceful tug with both her hands she removed the encrusted metal ball and threw it to the ground with all her might, aiming the stone towards it and a concentrated beam blasted it, destroying it completely. It smoked, disintegrating.

She desperately looked down at Olin Cian, who was breathing deeply and glaring down at the gaping wide hole in his body. It was raw, bloody and bleeding profusely. Kalantha took hold of Cian's shoulders and helped him to lie down. She removed her velvet satin blouse and tried to stop the bleeding with it. Cian reached up to stop her, and Ringo came closer and placed his paw upon the throbbing wound.

Reaching up, Olin placed her hands upon his temples. Waves of pain flew into her and she shook from it, shuddering. A green, glowing, sparkling light encompassed the two.

Olin ran his fingers over Kalantha's welted, scarred arm. The bloody gashed letters began to fade and heal over and away. He then took her hands in his own, sat up, and held them close to his heart.

"You will never lose me, Kalantha. It just isn't so. Beyond this illusion our bond will always be. You, I, Timothy, Ringo, all our energy, it just changes form but is always there." He softly, strongly whispered.

Olin then directed her hands down to the large, raw wound where Ringo had his paw. It glowed brightly, and started to close up and regenerate, as did all his bruises and cuts. The Superhero Figurines peeked out of her pocket, smiling, nodding, then ducked back.

"See-? The energy flows through you as it does me. It heals and protects."

All of Cian and Kalantha's wounds healed up and over. Cian slowly released Kalantha's hands and smiled to her, as Ringo licked his face.

"Thank you *again,* Kalantha," he deeply whispered.

Timothy, who was a bit away from them, stood halfway up, and searched his gaze in their direction shaking his head.

"Hey...what's going on? Is *he*-you know-is he still-

"No, he's doing fine," she said, smiling at Olin.

"*Oh.* Oh, Good," Tim voiced, still warily.

"You've got a really big headache, Timothy," Cian remarked, turning to him, rubbing his head and pointing over to him with the cane humorously. He even still had that cane.

Timothy tottered and stood, catching sight of Olin, waving his hands back and forth at him desperately.

"Wait a minute! No! NO! Last time you did that you-

A ray of violet light burst forth from Olin Cian's finger, and wrapped about Timothy's head. Cian pointed Kalantha's finger at Timothy and another ray of light contacted Tim, enveloping him in a healing haze.

Kalantha made a funny woozy face as if she was fainting, holding her head as she felt the pain Timothy had as well. Then they both placed their fingers down and with Ringo they made their way slowly over to Timothy. Cian started to examine him all over like a doctor would as Kalantha did to him.

"All right?" Cian commented, with a small smile.

"Yeah, yeah I am *now.* Thanks," Tim shyly said, giving him that funny long handshake again. Timothy quickly looked upward and paused, hearing something above him as well as feeling the vibrations. He noted a low flying vehicle shooting past them in the blackened sky.

It was swift and made a whistling sound. "What's THAT? It's NOT one of ours!" The ship came back around sharply, making another pass at them. "It's boomeranging BACK. We're being followed!"

The vehicle opened up and shot what seemed like three glowing red balls towards and down to them, and they all knew exactly what they were.

Olin Cian held his arms up and took a deep breath, concentrating, and a silvery arc of energy, a netted energy force field generated by him materialized, silvery, surrounding them all, deflecting the red glowing light balls. The ship fired once more and again, the shots deflected, and twisted towards the flying vehicle. They all made a direct hit, three big fireballs, throwing the ship off course, flinging it backwards, and spiraling downward to the ground. Within the distance it crashed, then eerily exploded, lighting up the dimmed horizon.

They all watched the explosion in silence. Kalantha reached to touch Cian's shoulder, and the Figurines in her back pocket cowered, peeking out, and ducked back inside.

"No one was aboard. Droned. It was all computer programmed. There will be more," Cian quietly spoke.

"There's always more." Timothy darkly commented, staring up at the sky. Mists were beginning to blow in, shrouding them in more mystic mystery. Kalantha watched the haze swirl about them.

"I feel... some kind of presence about. *Many* of them," she revealed, scanning the horizon.

"It's the Toppers." Cian revealed.

"He means Up-Toppers. Some of the inhabitants stay up here. It's not safe, but they want to. We help best we can," Timothy added. "I've known them for a while."

A distant echoing sound started up, the sound of a Bodhran drum eerily pounding out a beat repeatedly, an attention call. They were facing towards the West, and a bright, lighted flare shot up, illuminating the sky like a huge firework.

Ringo made an "ooohhh" sound, wondering at it. He knew it wasn't a bomb this time.

"Pretty, but not good news. It's a distress signal." Olin sighed out.

"Maybe they need more Miso seaweed soup, like we all do," Timothy tiredly mumbled, fatigued. Olin turned to him with a small smile, grateful for the joke.

"They need more than that. We have to get to them. Timothy, return to section eleven quickly and as fast as possible. We will meet up again, you'll know what to do; Tell them I'm ok, it's all clear and ready them for alert, and evacuation."

Timothy just stared at Olin silently, mouth hanging open. He shut it, giving him "the look."

"Olin Cian," He gritted, sternly, upset.

"Please listen and go,-*go*." He softly said, urgently.

Timothy crossed his large, muscled arms in defiance, distressed. Cian grabbed him and held him a moment, actually embracing him. A golden mist surrounded them.

"I honestly *can't believe you*. I'm not going to forget this, you know," Timothy emotively got out.

"I will contact you shortly," Cian said, as he pulled away, smiling at him.

"You aren't even going to tell me when, or... are you? If-*WHY?*" Tim miffed out.

"It's better that way, Tim, for safety's sake. It will not be for long. Stay away from those homers, you'll know anyway, *very soon.*"

"*Please,* don't make me leave. All of you *just got here,*" Tim mustered out, almost as if about to cry. He just didn't want to go, to leave them. Cian reached out to touch his shoulder gently.

"I shan't ever leave you, Timothy Ban Piobar. Thanks for the adventures, and jokes. It'll not be very long, you'll see."

Timothy peered over to his shoulder, which was glowing green where Cian had touched it, and moved back away from him. He lifted his glittery almond-golden eyes over to Kalantha, so solemn, and sad.

"Though at times he'll refuse it, take care of him," he spoke, hushed, winking.

"*Timothy*," Cian defensively chided, surprised, pulling Kalantha backwards with him.

Timothy was engulfed within a golden, brilliant light.

"You've waited seven and a half years for *her*, four since you met ME, possibly even longer and you will not even admit it, but *I WILL*. Like I said, I'm *not* going to forget this."

"YEAH!" Ringo barked out.

Timothy's bright golden light intensified, then changed to a blue-violet tinge, and quickly dwindled to just a hovering speck, and he...*vanished*.

Cian bowed his head in silence.

"...And *get out* of that awful outfit! *Good-bye!*" Tim's disembodied voice added.

Olin lifted his head slowly, glancing to Kalantha, blinking shyly. He slowly held his hand out to her. She stared at it, and grasped it firmly. Ringo grabbed onto the bottom cuff of Cian's black leathery bottoms with his teeth.

"*Don't let go*," he told her, strongly.

A golden, shimmery sparkling light enveloped them, and they all melted within it, swirling with the mists and fog; it turned into the blue violet haze, and they then slowly dissolved away...

Kalantha felt her body tingle, as if it had a mild form of pins and needles and then it numbed off. She only felt her hand holding Olins' and felt a spinning sensation. She thought, this must be what it felt like to be a "Transporter," to be able to do whatever it was they were doing, moving without even moving, only she didn't even have to meditate to do it.

She saw the energy vortex. She saw a bluish ball of light connected to her, and beside it another smaller one, just energy balls of light, not the physical forms of Olin Cian or Ringo.

Then she felt a sucking feeling, as if something was pushing her out from behind, like a wind force. She began to feel her physicality again, began to feel her heart beating and a hand holding onto her own. The sparkling misted energy faded off...

It was still just past dusk, misted, black, peeks of a sky and even some stars between the thick fog. Kalantha looked about her. It seemed to be... in front of her, some sort of village or camp.

There were old, mossy stone domed cottages with thatched roofs, and tents that seemed to be made with a coated burlap resin, Celtic symbols and swirled designs painted on top of them, as well as scattered bonfires and wooden carved posts that resembled totem poles but it wasn't Native American art-it was Celtic, and carved stones.

In the far distance she saw huge crumbling stone structures that must have been at one time some form of skyscraper, but they had been bombed and destroyed. They were futuristic, exquisite, arched and rounded, some pointed or vaulted even in their destruction art forms, yet no longer even usable.

The foggy, misted village in front of the ruins was lit by fiery torches all dotting about. She saw various hooded people lurking, huddled, and some form of domesticated animals, yet they seemed *mutated, really wild as if bits and pieces of them were just stuck on to different parts of other animals...freaky Frankenstein creatures...*

Larger farm animals and other creatures ambled in the dimness, looking half-normal, half-something *else*-either the animals had evolved to somehow deal with the poisoned atmosphere, she thought, or they had been malformed because OF it. Some of them even looked vaguely familiar, as if she had seen them from somewhere but couldn't figure it out. But they were being cared for. Some kind of looked like horses. One or two were genuinely huge Clydesdales. The others looked like they were half elephant, almost cartoonish; the other ones could be cows but had longer necks and legs like giraffes with horns or really long disproportionate legs.

She just couldn't make it out, what they actually *were* or could *be* but they were *alive,* and she did see the gigantic rat or rodent scuttle across the dirt path into the patch of huge hedges on the side of them... she heard Ringo growl a bit as it hunkered past them.

In front of her, some of the "Uptoppers" were grouped and standing about a bonfire, stirring a huge pot kettle of soup or stew, holding out bowls and pottery plates for a meal. They all at once turned their heads at the misty golden light appearing in front of them and reacted vocally to it in wonder and amazement, yet unafraid. An older man pointed at it, at them.

"Blessed be! 'Tis the Gods arrivin'! I told ye he'd **come!** It's *Olin Cian!* 'Tis HE!" He blurted.

"Yes, SirVaul McHeartwee, He must've seen the flare, the Beacon!" An older woman Uptopper exclaimed to the older man, who seemed to be the leader of the clan.

Kalantha, Olin Cian and Ringo solidified in front of the Bonfire, as a wolfish howl permeated the air.

"*Oh, Another* is with him. Oh, a GODDESS she is! Rare and ripe with the fruit of truth! Look at them! And they have their own spirit animal with them!" The older man exclaimed.

The older man, SirVaul McHeartwee approached them, bowing deeply, addressing them with gracious pleasure. "Welcome, venerable one."

Olin Cian smiled grandly, pulled the man up from his bow and hugged him, as Ringo bowed back to him. Kalantha followed the greeting and graced a deep curtsy to them, not wanting to offend. A pink, auric light beamed out from Cian as he embraced the man, as his energy transferred to him. The Uptoppers reacted in awe, murmuring.

Cian moved closer, to talk with the group. Kalantha and Ringo followed behind him, closer to the huge, flickering bonfire.

"The Extirpators have been pillaging you again. They were looking for *me*. I humbly ask your forgiveness and you need assistance. How may Kalantha, Ringo and I be of help to you?"

The Uptoppers all murmured to each other, still in stupefied shock that Cian, Kalantha and Ringo were in front of them and wished to help them in person. The older man who greeted them was pushed forward by the rest to speak to them.

"Welcome back to our home, *Talamh Piobar*. The "*Gorm Granna*," they will come once more, using their evil ways and glas bombs, destroying whatever is left of our village. They... are *not human*, they have NO HEART, and seems like no soul as well. We do not know WHAT they be! Your Capitan Sergeant, Timothy Ban Piobar, had forewarned us and said he would be back."

"Gorm Granna? Not *human?* Are-are they something *living?*" Kalantha inquired.

Funny, she had this strange feeling about this older man, as if she recognized him. The salient eyebrows, the eyes, *that face,* even though he was much older and had a very long, unkept braided beard and mustache and really long, plaited hair... especially *his voice*, which was-some kind of UK accent, a bit of a mix of Irish too... Scouse...? Liverpool? No... just no, couldn't be him-*could it*?

Cian turned to Kalantha, whispering.

"It seems the Extirpators have *created* it. It's a mystically formed Illusion that has turned living, *alive*. It's called a *Tulpa,* a kind of thought-form. Remember what the council members, what they *did to me* in the sub?"

"You mean they think together and it collects and manifests, and comes to *life?* A *thought creation?*" She whispered back, still eyeing the old Uptopper.

"Yes, Kalantha; It is called a Tulpa. Only I believe this one to be *far worse*. I–kind of wound up doing it *too,* inadvertently. I guess I was getting a bit lonely waiting for you and I do get lonely, you know, and was meditating about man's best friend, thinking how nice it would be, to have someone special to talk to and, ah, I opened my eyes after the meditation and, well, *Ringo* was just there staring at me..."

"You mean you created RINGO? He's a Tulpa?" She amazingly muttered.

"*What do you mean?*" Ringo squeaked, perturbed.

"He has *no idea,* shhh. You've done *it too,* you know." Cian mumbled back to her.

"*I have?* Wait-what have *I done?*"

Cian placed his fingers to his lips in the shush position and became more serious, turning to the Uptoppers.

"Your people, their lives are no longer *safe* here." He told them.

"*Not safe,*" Ringo barked.

The Older Uptopper man, SirVaul, with the salient eyebrows and accent, now noticeably distressed, stared down to Ringo incredulously, at a talking dog, then to Cian.

"But this is OUR WAY, Our Talamh Piobar! " he declared, frazzled, stubbornly.

"I understand how important this all is to you, your village Talamh Piobar, and all that you have lived for and fought for and survived through. Whatever is left of what is decided to give to you. But soon, *here,* **nothing** of Talamh Piobar will be *left,*" Olin gently but gravely revealed.

"But YE are here t'aid us," the Older Uptopper woman voiced.

"*Yes*, I-WE are, we *will* help you."

"AND yer *CLOTHES,* Tch Tch!" she pointed to them, glaring at Olin Cian funny, strangely, gesturing towards his unappealing attire, coming up to him and touching it and shaking her head dis-approvingly. Cian was still in the tight, black leathery, bat-winged metallic suit the *"others"* had dressed him into.

"I-sorry...sorry; forgive the fashion offense I had a detour before coming around. There was no time to change." He apologized.

The Uptopper woman then turned towards Kalantha.

"Tch tch, Ye should do well with a spare change a' garments TOO. An WHO by chance dressed YE?"

Kalantha thumbed over to Olin Cian, giving him the true blame who just shrugged sheepishly.

"It figures. A Goddess should be *dressed* as one, fer respect's sake!"

"Go follow Culghanor Righbe to the tent yonder. She'll be givin' ye what's needed. 'Tis a rare an' wondrous sight of night it is. Take heed to care for them, Culghanor." The older Uptopper Man SirVaul told them, nodding, gathering his minions at the ready.

The older woman, Culghanor Righbe started to lead them to the tent.

"I think 'tis *them* who'll be takin' care of *us* soon, SirVaul. Please, do follow."

The older woman Uptopper Culghanor led them down a small path towards the large Celtic decorated tent structure, as various other Uptoppers peered out of their dwellings and stared at them, playing music from handmade instruments, flutes, drums, fiddles, a hand harp and squeeze box.

It seemed they were anticipating the heralded event. They were all joyeous, respectful and very happy to see them. A small little girl, about six years old, tattled behind them curiously as Culghanor opened the flap to the tent and they all followed in, as well as the little girl.

Inside the tent dwelling stood old wooden Gaelic furnishings, amazingly carved artwork and rustic living antiquities. The woman Culghanor Righbe crossed to an old bark wood cabinet scrawled in Celtic designing. It seemed a sacred piece, draped with ornate satin silky swaths of material.

Culghanor spotted the little girl who tattled behind them. She reached inside the cabinet and pulled out two whitish-blue bundles of linen, with fancy accessories and intricate sewn needlework, and handed them to the little girl, who turned towards Cian, Kalantha and Ringo.

"We knew ye would be comin' an' prepared, legend told us such. Go ahead, lil' lassie, ye snuck in t' see them, go ahead an' meet them now."

The little girl, with long, intricately plaited red hair, timidly walked over to them, holding out the two folded linen outfits, pure bluish-white and gold, intricate Celtic designs, needlework and trimmings, all hand done and with great care, traditional and historic Ulster cycle type garments of high quality, made for what seemed to be royalty.

Culghanor snatched up some lace tie up boots from the floor near a mounded, straw mattress covered with a warm, Celtic quilt rimmed with some type of fur.

"Please, accept our gifts, for your grace and heartfelt compassion." She pleaded. The little girl laid the outfits atop the quilted straw mattress and curtsied as Culghanor Righbe set the boots down as well and curtsied, tying a special braided Celtic scarf about Ringo's neck, in likeness to the bracelets Kalantha had seen on Timothy. Ringo licked her hand.

Olin looked down upon the outfits starkly with a strange expression, very silent.

The old woman, Culghanor then crossed over to Kalantha and hugged her. The little girl scampered over and hugged Olin's legs. A surge of pink auric light burst out from all of them, and around them, shining. Culghanor and the little girl gasped and backed out of the tent in shock, closing the flap.

Olin continued to stare oddly at the outfits lain out upon the mattress. He slowly moved over, quietly sat down upon the bed in half lotus, one leg placed over the other, close to cross-legged.

Ringo trotted over to him and jumped up between the two piles of clothes. Olin once again looked down at the clothing, and his hand reached out to run his fingers gently over the piles and they trembled, clutching them tightly in a strong fist for a moment. He glared at the linen gifts hauntingly, an emotion never really shown with him, for it seemed nostalgic and rather emotively... *human.*

Kalantha watched him do this, not saying a word. He then turned his gaze to stare over at *her* in the very same way. His stare and his eyes were a myriad of untold secret emotions, but he said nothing of them. He did speak up, though, in a strangely humorous way.

"We could end our lives here for this now, just letting you know. It's our choice. It wouldn't make a difference. You still would not lose me. We can't back out of it and it would be highly insulting not to take the gifts. They'd write us up as an epic poem and we'd honorably or dishonorably go down in history, literally. Down."

Kalantha slowly walked to him, sitting to the side silently, tentative. She slowly reached over and unfastened the metallic plated top chest vest Olin Cian has on over the leathery suit and slid it off of him, and the strange stretchy black top came right off with it.

She picked up the linen tunic top from a clothing pile that seemed to be his, and placed it on him and over his torso, lacing up the front ties, saying absolutely nothing.

Olin softly slipped off what was left of the velvet blouse Kalantha had on and gently laid it down, picking up the linen gown from "her" pile and slipping it over her head as she slid it down over her leotard, stepping out of the britches and her stockings.

The hidden Superhero figurines scrambled out of the back pocket of the britches and up the back of her dress, as Olin tied a braided, gold-blue belt sash with a pouch sewn into it about her waist and shoulder from behind very tenderly, intensely. The Figurines secretly climbed into it.

Suddenly Cian pulled Kalantha close, holding her strongly, with his arm around her waist and the other around her shoulder and neck, with gentle magnetic force, also slinging the cylinder plans about her. He actually stroked her hair, eyes closed, leaning his head against hers tenderly with affection.

Kalantha was a bit surprised by the attracted, devoted action, but she reached back to tenderly touch his cheek, and hugged him back. More pink auric sparkling light burst forth from them.

Then-she *felt it*. Kalantha felt something... *expansive, and ominously huge*, and gasped.

"*They* just *hit* section Eleven, all have been evacuated. *Tim,* he's with the networkers, he made it out with everyone. He's all right," Olin softly revealed, just as an immense rumble was felt and heard under and about them.

Objects inside of the tent rattled and shuddered, and more rumbles permeated after.

The Uptoppers outside were heard vocalizing reactions of fear and anger. Ringo yelped, jumping off of the mattress.

Kalantha turned to face him and the look on his face said it all.

"You mean the center? *Your* center? Your Network? The one the plans were made for?"

Cian made a short quick shake of his head. He knelt down and flipped off Kalantha's boots and replaced them with the laced, linen ones. She sat down upon the mattress as he started to tie them up.

"We must help these people lovie, do whatever we can for them. We are all the hope to them. Timothy will be returning with the rest soon. Until then, it is only Us."

Ringo cleared his throat. Olin looked to him and winked. Kalantha made a move to stop Cian's actions of lacing.

"Let me do that."

Cian continued dressing her feet subserviently as he spoke.

"I shan't leave your side. If we must separate, concentrate and just think upon my name. The stone might help, too."

Cian finished lacing her boots and stood, smiling warmly at her. He pulled off his black footwear and sock type garments and made a motion to undo the stretchy pant garments to slip on the rest of his outfit but then looked down at them and stopped abruptly; Kalantha stared over to him, then reacted after realizing why he stopped dressing. Ringo gave a loud snicker, and so did the Figurines peeking out the pouch.

"*Oh*, "*They*" didn't give you any underwear," she comically commented.

Cian shrugged, then sniffed.

"Same thing happened the last time. It's rather comfortable you see and-

Kalantha cut in on him as she scooped up his linen pants, throwing them at him, as well as the undergarments built into them and he caught them.

"I don't have any EITHER. That's what you get for forgetting to give some to ME. All you gave me were those velvet tights and *this* leotard."

"Right. Undergarments are kind of in short supply here lovie."

They both shook their heads and turned about, not facing one another. Kalantha scooped up the rare, one-piece bodice undergarment given to her and hitched it up under her long, tunic dress and boots, while unsnapping the side snaps of the leotard and tights, allowing her to take them off, as Cian did the same with his black leg garment, then both turning back towards each other politely.

Kalantha then picked up a silken linen blue sash and wrapped it about Cian's long tunic top, tying it, helping him into his boots as he had done with her.

"Olin, would I still have met you if I hadn't transported here?" She quietly asked him; still wrapping his boots about his linen pant bottoms.

"Yes, still."

The bodhran drumrolls and shouting noises outside the tent grew louder, furious, with screams and war cries, chants of *"Gorm Granna!"*

Kalantha stared back up at Olin Cian nervously and trembled. She felt-felt as if a strange, old door had been opened in the back of her mind, and she was going backward, way, way back, feeling things far beyond where she was now. She made a small gasp and clutched his leg and held it strongly...she began to actually mumble in an old, ancient Gaelic tongue language incoherently, as if in a trance once more. Cian touched the top of her head and stroked it, reaching down and hugged her back.

"Mhm-yes, I figured some old memories would come out, Kalantha. Work through it, from long and far ago but it was a special time for us, it will pass soon. You were my Cushlah Macree, remembering me that way is heartbreaking," he whispered gently to her.

Kalantha was recollecting a life time, trying hard to keep her composure but the surroundings surged everything back into her memory and triggered it, as before in the submarine...

"That's what you used to call me **here**-Oh...we *died* here, *together*, that life I saw, the one with us running in the forest... we had just had our marriage vows secretly...they were so afraid of our...mystic abilities... they thought it was dark magic... we were able to do very close to what we can now and it frightened them and they-it's flowing back, who you were to me when I-" she sighed, brokenly. "*I don't like this...*"

"It's okay, you were the pulse o' me heart, you always will be, you were always so strong. You can get through this, we can do this, okay? We have to go out there."

Kalantha straightened up, still mumbling in old Gaelic oddly, and let out a short breath. Olin Cian comforted her and looked at her wonderingly.

"This-is HARD. That memory... I can see how you even LOOKED back then...." She whispered.

She was staring at him, and he was... Cian was blurring, morphing into another man from ancient Gaelic time, strong, tall, handsome, still fair, in war clothing and a medicine man bag, a healer warrior, then he morphed back again, back to looking like Olin Cian once more. It switched on and off a few times until it steadied back to just Olin Cian once more.

"I know, lovie; Let's go do this, Kalantha. We can do this and turn this around, save what we can." Kalantha nodded, took a deep breath and shook it off; she grabbed his hand and pulled him towards the tent exit, as Ringo followed them. "You want a good luck hug and kiss?" he mumbled to her.

"Nope; You just gave me the hug and already gave me the *kiss,* unfortunate you had no idea you did it or felt it; You're honestly a good kisser, not bad, charmingly endowed I saw all of you in your birthday suit glory when they were extirpating you on that table," she slyly commented, hauling him out the door. "Anyway, I need something to look forward to when we finish."

Olin Cian gave her a stunned, embarrassed stare, and then looked out, as if to peer at *"us"* in a tiff at being humorously rejected, and because he missed feeling the kiss as well ...Ringo snickeringly giggled and they flew out the flap of the tent...

Chapter Nine

K alantha led Olin Cian and Ringo out of the tent, to see the Uptoppers all running about eclectically and gathering what essentials they could carry and pack, rounding up their odd menagerie of mutated animal/beings, and ushering the little ones together. Kalantha noted it was the first time she had seen a multitude of young children, and they looked at the most rather healthy.

The Uptoppers seemed to not to be affected as much with the "elderly condition"; they were more robust than the city dwellers she had seen and had age ranges. The men were large and the women fierce, of all nationalities and all of them had painted their faces with war paint and were screaming cries of battle, waving torches. It seemed to her like she was thrown backwards to the very old ways of Gaelic Ulster Ireland, and these people had kept that tradition or had someway adopted it, ignoring the high tech advanced evolution and instead honed and tapped within the mystic magical energy of the earth, of the ancients as their very own.

Then she understood why *Timothy* was who *he was.* He was *one of them*, living with them and the network since arriving here to help them, but he was a mix of it all. He had used everything Cian had taught him to help this section of humans within reason of allowance integrating himself as one of them.

More heavy mist and fog had rolled in, and it was hard to see everyone's actions yet you could hear them. Olin Cian moved quickly, approaching the large, grassed rocky clearing near the bonfire, Ringo right behind. He could hear the villagers all getting ready, bravely taking a stand for what little they even had.

Kalantha, at his side, both stood very still and stopped; they both turned their gaze upward simultaneously, as three low flying vehicles had appeared, circling above them, weaving in and out of the dense cloud cover, their search lights beaming in and out of the foggy mist. Some things seemed to drop out of the ships, things that were very large and green, and something hugely round and blue...

Olin glanced over at Kalantha, and she to he, both reacting simultaneously as if they were connected and one person, tensely, and nodded to each other.

A song blared out, from Olin Cian's universal stereo system... guitar riff wailing... Ringo screamed with it...

Cian's automatic speaker system was even built in to the Uptopper camp, and it was feeding off of their thoughts...

"Revolution" ... it played throughout the entire incident...

"You say you want a revolution
Well, you know
We all want to change the world
You tell me that it's evolution
Well, you know
We all want to change the world
But when you talk about destruction
Don't you know that you can count me out...
Don't you know it's gonna be
All right, all right, all right
You say you got a real solution
Well, you know
We'd all love to see the plan
You ask me for a contribution
Well, you know
We're doing what we can

But if you want money for people with minds that hate
All I can tell is brother you have to wait....
Don't you know it's gonna be
All right, all right, all right...
You say you'll change the constitution
Well, you know
We all want to change your head
You tell me it's the institution
Well, you know
You better free you mind instead
But if you go carrying pictures of chairman Mao
You ain't going to make it with anyone anyhow...
Don't you know it's gonna be
All right, all right, all right
All right, all right, all right
All right, all right, all right
All right, all right..."

OLIN CIAN'S RIGHT ARM and hand shot upward with Kalantha's left, and their fingers entwined with a mudra fist above their heads.

A dazzling blast of light burst forth from their fisted fingers and arched above and about them all, around the *entire* Uptopper Camp, encircling them as a protective shield, an intertwined, honey-combed, hexagon plaited shaped net shining over it all, yet the thread, the threadlike beams of light that formed it were written and linked in letters and sentences... over and over, "ALL YOU NEED IS LOVE"...

It was crisscrossed in lighted pink beams. It was amazing. From the clouds above, mysterious, thick, saturated blue mist started to twirl, trickle and descend upon them and all over the area...

It was followed by a dark, foreboding legion of carolers, a caste of disembodied voices permeated the air about them, even louder than the music, interloping, looping over and over, and the strange grating sound of chattering TEETH...?

"STOP WITH YOUR BLASTED MUSIC! STOP IT! YOU WILL NOT LAST LONG...LAST LONG... THERE IS NO ESCAPE... NO ESCAPE... WE HAVE YOU AND WILL CAPTURE YOU AGAIN UNTIL YOU ARE ONE WITH US...WITH US... WITH USSS... YOUR MUSIC WILL DIE! TALAMH PIOBAR WILL BE NO MORE!"

"MY MUSIC? Is that what this is all about? My music is the only thing that *stops* you from attacking! It is full of love FOR you! I WAS with you, I still AM. You have betrayed yourselves, and decided not to fight it off, fight off the "others." Now you are with them, a part of them. Time is so precious to you. How many more lives as you see them must it take now to extinguish this deed? Quite a few, you know. Allow me... allow me to *HELP YOU*," Olin Cian threw out to the voices. They interrupted, again with the strange sound of chattering TEETH... more blue mist swirled above and about them...

"WE HAVE MADE NO MISTAKE! *YOU* HAVE! YOU WILL PAY DEARLY...PAY DEARLY! SHE WILL BE TAKEN FROM YOU, *JEREMY HILARY BOOB, PHD,* AND WHAT WE DESIRE YOU WILL CREATE...NO MORE MUSIC! YOU WILL DO OUR BIDDING! YOU WILL DO AS WE COMMAND YOU...AND YOUR MUSIC WILL BE NO MORE!"

"Jeremy Hilary Boob, Ph.D.?" Ringo confusedly questioned.

"Jeremy Hilary Boob, P.H.D..." Kalantha echoed, managing to say, eyeing Cian weirdly. "Is that-is that really your *name?*"

"That's what *"THEY"* call me," the *"Gorm Granna,"* Cian whispered.

"I told you, he's the *Nowhere man,"* Ringo whined.

"Oh my-O*h my God*... I think I *know* what's *going on* now..." Kalantha mumbled, under her breath."I think I know who "THEY" are! Have you ever SEEN them, Olin? Have you ever really *seen* the "*others?*""

Cian shook his head at her, and was about to try to answer, but the Booming voices about them stopped abruptly and became incoherent howling.

Another burst of bright light blazed forth from Olin and Kalantha's hands and it shot up overhead, expanding upon the blue-misted haze. The Blue lights about them dissipated into blobs, forming 11 blue spheres, surrounding them all in a circle.

The blue spinning spheres expanded, materializing into robed dark blue forms with appendages and limbs. The arms of the forms swirled and extended towards them. Saturated blue, threadlike swirls unraveled from the hands with a thunderous cackling noise, like lighting.

Above, formulating with the entire spectacle in the heavens, was now hovering an immense, circular, pastel-lemon yellow flying vehicle descending, coming down from the low hanging cloud cover. It was alike the underwater transport vehicle, only much, much larger.

Kalantha glared up at it, mouth hanging open. It was an enormous high tech "flying saucer," only it was actually decorated and in close resemblance to a round, futuristic cartoonish "*yellow submarine*"...

A lavender beam of light illuminated downward from it, upon it all.

"*It's Tim*," Cian muttered.

The tendrils that undulated out of the eleven hooded forms turned into a neon brilliant blue, a web-like structure like the one Cian had formed as their force field, only this one was all shaped like lightning bolts, weaving in and out of them like a spider web, trapping them. They glowed and buzzed with electrified energy, intensifying, winding in and about all their bodies and honeycombed force field, but not touching them.

"Do not move, Kalantha, Ringo... do not move, at all," Olin softly instructed.

Above them, the monstrous, hovering lemon yellow ship opened some hatches and some transport "bubbled" structures descended from it, like the one that had scooped up Cian in the sea, with attached long, snaking, lighted red pipes. They hit the grounds about them and slid open.

They watched all the Uptoppers and their weird animals start to scramble into them with whatever they could haul with them, coming out of hiding, not before launching a few arrows and airborne fire torches at the web like, blue lightning trap about Ringo, Kalantha and Olin Cian, screaming war cries of "Gorm Granna" once more, attempting to help free them.

They were all able to rush into the transports and the lighted snaky pipes started retracting to haul them upward into the gigantic flying "yellow spaceship submarine," safely rescuing the entire Uptopper camp.

A voice echoed out from the flying space vehicle and clouds, *Timothy's voice*, on a huge speaker com-link...

"I'VE GOT THEM ALL, JUST GOTTA GET YOU GUYS NOW. WAIT! WHAT THE-? *OH MY GOD...*"

Above and to the side of Timothy's ship and coming downward, had been dropped huge *green apples* and an *immense blue bubble*. They started to swing over and make their way down towards Olin Cian, Kalantha and Ringo, *and* towards Tim's humungous flying vehicle ... *to capture them all...*

"Tim, don't try anything," Cian warned, calling up and out.

Down below, the 11 robed beings' hoods and robes started slipping off... and they were all *laughing*...

Every single one of the 11... was a BLUE MEANIE... "Gorm Granna" in Gaelic.

All of the different types of them were represented and there: The Chief, Max, the mascot, Storm bloopers, the butterfly stompers, the countdown clowns, the tall apple bonkers, the hidden persuaders, the snapping turtle turks, the jack o' nippers, the four-headed bulldog... the anti music missile was already above them... they were *alive and real,* very real, bodily real, not cartoons...the only one of the Blue Meanies that wasn't there was...ah...

"DO YOU SEE WHAT I'M SEEING? I DON'T BELIEVE THIS! I HAVE TO GET YOU OUT OF HERE!" Tim's voice boomed out.

"Set co-ordinates 0-5-7-3300, Tim. GO!" Cian yelled out.

"OLIN, DAMN YOU, WHY ARE YOU DOING THIS? COME WITH US! C'MON! YOU'RE GONNA GET APPLE BONKED!"

"Because I have to. You will understand," Cian loudly said back, as Ringo started to growl and he gazed over to Kalantha.

"I REALLY HOPE SO. I GUESS I SHOULDN'T BE ASKING WHEN I'D SEE YOU AGAIN." Tim's voice bellowed out again.

"Soon enough, not to worry. Tend to the Uptoppers for now, and pass what you have learned. You'll see, and be happy. Get out of here before that blue bubble traps the ship! Keep playing the music, mate!" Olin remarked.

"YOU HAPPEN TO NEED SOME DEFENDING YOURSELF! WHAT THE HELL...IS THAT REALLY-? ARE-ARE THEY FOR REAL? THEY'RE *BLUE MEANIES*!" Tim's voice echoed once more.

"*Blue meanies! Blue meanies! That four-headed bulldog is gonna kill me I thought of him, too! I'm sorry, I'm sorry!*" Ringo barked out.

"Shush, Ringo. It's A Tulpa. A thought form created and manifested by others and fears, just a bunch of thoughts... they're tapping into what I and you and Kalantha, and Timothy had been thinking of. They can change their forms and create them just like we can. And it's very real mate. *Don't interfere,* Timothy. As the *Captain, and a Sergeant, Maorsháirsint, Captaen,* they will go *after* you," Cian dreadfully declared.

"THEN YOU ARE REALLY IN FOR IT! DON'T TAKE TOO LONG. I'M IN THE MOOD FOR GRANNY SMITH APPLESAUCE, THOUGH, SORRY. THEY AREN'T GETTING ME! OR YOU! RINGO, HELP ME OUT HERE!" Tim's voice blared out.

Ringo snorted, then looked up to the pouch hanging from Kalantha with the Superhero figurines peeping out from it. Luke and the Wolverine dropped something floppy down to Ringo, and Ringo grabbed it with his mouth. It was a round, black circle, a *"hole."*

Ringo flung it upward, it grew in size and it flew through the blue lightning and pink lettered glowing netting, all the way up to the big blue bubble, sticking there, creating a "hole" in it.

Globs of gooey goop started to plop down out of it, draining the bubble. Timothy's behemoth yellow vehicle beamed a huge lavender lightning bolt beam at the gigantic flying green apples, blasting them to mush... it all started to rain down about them.

Captaen Timothy's ship then vanished within the misty clouds...

Kalantha stared at all the mush and glop dropping from the sky... she was wearying, the energy she was putting into the force field was draining her life force greatly and she squinted, sweaty, pining, trying to stay up and awake. She was feeling very faint. Olin noticed her condition as the blue lighting beams intensified, and the Blue Meanies around them danced around crazily...all of them, as if in some tribal triumph dance. She heard Olin's voice telepathically in her mind...

Kalantha, lovie, hold on, do not move, do not make a sound now. The sensor beams will detect it and you can be taken if I am not

careful. They can physically slice through you. Please, concentrate...
concentrate on the stone...

Kalantha, even through her waning consciousness did what was asked of her, and the stone about her neck glowed brilliantly. Another surge of energized light blasted from Cian and Kalantha's entwined fist, and strong light rays of green burst forth from the stone, eating away at the blue lightning webbing, disintegrating them. They fizzled and melted away.

Kalantha made a short gasp and crumpled, collapsing into Olin's arms, limp. The pink "ALL YOU NEED IS LOVE," glowing web still remained, shining brightly.

"Thank you, Cushlah Macree," he whispered lovingly to her unmoving form, holding her tightly.

The Blue Meanie beings howled and screeched, defeated, hissing at Cian, Ringo and the now unconscious Kalantha, wriggling their tongues, chattering their teeth, and tightening their circle.

Cian looked at them all closing in on him with a small, intriguing smile. He then... snapped his finger straight at the Chief Blue Meanie... *His Blueness*, smiling...

"Arise, arise, arouse, a rose, a rosey nose!" Cian comically whispered...

And... a *flower* spurted forth from his Bluenesses' big, long nose, as if growing there.

The Chief screeched, shaking his head and huge proboscis with the bloom sprouting up from it.

"Well, it had worked before...I guess you all aren't ready for peace yet..."

His Blueness the Chief Blue Meanie howled at him excitedly and jumped up and down like a toddler having a violent temper tantrum, as more roses sprouted all over him, showing Olin the unfortunate answer he wished not to hear or see.

Olin sighed and gave a small frown, disappointed he couldn't have a badly needed truce yet and figured he'd just have to wait and then peered down, backing up a few steps, still holding Kalantha who was unmoving. Ringo backed up with him, snickering. The Superhero figurines poked up and out of her pouch, nodding to Cian, agreeing with his flower choice mischievously and he nodded back. He tapped his boot upon a small stone, and he, Kalantha, her hitchers and Ringo disappeared within and down a shaft of blue violet sparkling light in split second speed as the hole plugged up above them tightly...

Olin Cian, Kalantha and Ringo materialized and shot downward into an awaiting underground yellow transport vehicle, much alike the large ship Tim was piloting, only much smaller, just a two-seater. Cian gently placed a still fainted out Kalantha into one of the front seats, strapping her in, Ringo between them. The doors auto closed on them.

Sitting in a seat adjacent to hers, Cian turned on the controls with a wave of his palm, and the view screen panel facing them lit up. He entered codes on the typing panels with more lightning speed as a purple light illuminated the interior. Cian grabbed the steering mechanism, strapped into the seat, pulling around some straps to secure Ringo. He hit a button and they blasted forward within a long, dark, tubular exit tunnel in high velocity.

The view screen in front of him sharpened, and within it was the scene of the interior of the cockpit of a huge, round, light yellow flying ship, with Timothy overseeing and giving orders, it seeming like a cartoon version of their real life, only in flesh and blood. Timothy stopped where he was, and looked over and out remotely, sensing something, facing the view screen.

"*Olin Cian... Olin Cian?*" he mumbled, in disbelief.

Cian turned up the volume on the com-link, staring at the screen.

"Hey mate... Timothy?" he replied, as his vehicle shot forward even faster.

Timothy, on the view screen, walked closer precariously, closely staring into the screen at Olin Cian. He had this incredulous face on, eyes wide.

*"**You Knew;** You always **knew**. I can only imagine what else you know about us and it all..."* Timothy ventured to say. He looked closely, leaning into the screen, spotting Kalantha."Will Kalantha be all right?" He remarked, dotingly.

Cian turned to Kalantha, who was sitting in the seat opposite next to him with Ringo. Her eyes were closed. He moved over closer to her and encircled his arm tenderly around her shoulder, and Ringo licked her cheek.

On the view screen, Timothy, some of his crew members, and various Uptoppers, among them the Older man with the salient eyebrows, SirVaul and Culghanor, the older lady, as well as the little red-haired braided girl in his ship all crowded about him, into the view screen to take a look at them, and they sighed.

"That's more like it. She'll be fine. Uh, what about those other ships that were circling above you before?" Timothy's voice wavered on the com-link.

"They're still up there. As soon as we break through they'll try something. They cannot go after you, don't worry."

On the view screen, the Uptoppers around Timothy made a huge ruckus, playing Celtic music and celebrating, merrymaking in the large cockpit cabin, waving at Olin Cian.

"Well O'course they can't, your co-ordinates tripped us all backwards in time. We literally rode the akashic record, flipped into the Ireland Ulster Cycle Era. Pretty neat trick. How did you do it?" Timothy remarked.

"Anything is possible, just not permanent. I thought the Toppers would be more comfortable there." Olin answered, quiet.

"I best believe they are ecstatic, Olin Cian. Thanks mate," Tim managed to get out, almost being drowned by the Uptopper music and shouting.

A small sigh and hiccup escaped from Kalantha, and she was waking up and coming to. Cian stifled a laugh and hugged her. Ringo softly smacked her face again with his tongue as the Celtic music drifted from the intercom, mingling with the song starting up in Cian's vehicle:

"All Together now..."

Cian's light yellow submarine cloned vehicle broke out of the underground tunnel and shot right out, straight up to the sky, very high into the clouds, transforming into a flyer, lights blinking on the wings and nose lighting the way. As soon as it leveled out, red light balls swarmed in and attempted to attack it. The vehicle dodged them and shot even faster. In the distance, a dim lineup of some kind of another flying vehicle was forming... and multiplying, like a plague of flying insects...

"One two three four
Can I have a little more....

"FIVE, SIX SEVEN EIGHT nine ten..." Kalantha counted the forming vehicles, in time with the lyrics...

Five six seven eight nine ten
I love you...."

"All in all, I would say it would be twenty-seven hundred mosquitos to one," Cian mumbled, as he steered the flyer, counting the forming dots on the radar view screen... they looked like huge mosquitos...

Ringo sighed sadly.

"A B C D
Can I bring my friend to tea
E F G H I J
I love you...."

"THEY'RE FORMING A CIRCLE and surrounding us," Kalantha whispered, futilely.

Bom bom bom bompa bom
Sail the ship Bompa bom
Chop the tree bompa bom
Skip the rope bompa bom
Look at me..."

"NO LIFE FORMS ON THE ships, they are all run by computers and drones. They sure like imitating other life forms. I can feel they are using way too much power, though, they-

"WE WILL DESTROY YOU, JEREMY, AND YOUR CUSHLAH MACREE AND SCRAPPY MUTT TOO! YOU ARE SURROUNDED WITH NO WAY OUT! DIVINE SPECK YOU SHALL BE NO MORE!"

Horrible cackling voices interrupted on the com-link, with teeth chattering.

"All together now
All together now..."

"DID THEY JUST CALL me a MUTT?" Ringo growled, unbelieving...

"YES!" The Superhero figurines squealed back at him, popping out of the pouch on Kalantha's dress belt...

Kalantha glared down and *finally saw* them and reacted, kind of as you would think she would... The Luke figure waved to her, and the Wolverine bumped his shoulder and pulled him back down into the pouch.

Kalantha... said absolutely nothing she just couldn't believe it... Olin Cian glanced at the radar screen, then outward in front of the window out the ship, sighing.

"I *told you* that you created something TOO, didn't I?" Cian humorously commented to Kalantha. Kalantha shockingly glared down at her belt pouch, then to Cian, who smiled and shrugged...

"You better think FAST, divine speck," she swiftly humored back.

"Got it." Cian pulled hard upon the steering mechanism...

"Black white green red
Can I take my friend to bed
Pink brown yellow orange and blue
I love you..."

THE FLYING VEHICLE dropped straight downward, plunging, as the circle of droned ships coming towards them which were shaped and created like huge mechanical metallic droned mosquitos, and started firing blasts of more screaming red glowing balls and laser lightning bolt blasts from their elongated proboscis labium, scrolling in and out.

But instead in a fluke of true luck, they all started to hit and smash into each other and ended in massive explosions of scrambled mosquito parts and fake red spurting blood dripping, floating everywhere...an insect graveyard, totally missing Cian's flyer.

"All together now
All together now
All together now..."

"Hey,That was a good one; rather gruesome. Didn't think you had it in you," Timothy's voice fluted out from the com-link, as the view screen showed the excited Uptoppers and Timothy whooping and hollering behind him happily.

"Well, something had to be done. Nobody was inside the ships, um, the mosquitos. I feel best about that issue," Cian replied back, still flying.

"Ah sure, sure, you just obliterated their entire defense line in one shot!" Tim proudly proclaimed on the com-link.

Olin Cian's smile faded as he continued staring out the front window of the flyer strangely...

"Well, mate, seems there's still one more thing LEFT...or RIGHT... we all almost forgot about," Cian's wavering voice remarked, eyes wide.

Timothy and the Uptoppers all crowded around the view screen, peering into it suspiciously.

"Huh? What's that?"

Shouts of surprise and shock came from the intercom, even a strangled laugh...

"Er, **this...**" Olin said, as he stared out in front of the window calmly....

Outside, dead ahead and hovering, was the huge, monstrous, grinning, dreadful ***BLUE FLYING GLOVE...***

"Bom bom bom bompa bom
Sail the ship Bompa bom
Chop the tree bompa bom
Skip the rope bompa bom
Look at me..."

THE UPTOPPERS TOOK one look and started screaming "Gorm Etil Miotog!" Over and over again...

"*Are you kidding me?*" Timothy blurted, unbelieving.

"Anything is possible. It's most probably another Tulpa, but it's *real* all right..."

The Dreadful **Blue Flying Glove** started laughing, a booming, dark, loud laugh at them, starting to shoot right towards them...

Ringo gasped, Kalantha just stunningly stared at it, the Wolverine's fist popped out from the pouch with the claws open, and Luke' s Light saber flicked up on, sticking out the pouch as well...

"*Will you look at the size of–could it really have been that large in the-? I guess so. You and your anything's possible!*" Timothy's voice nervously commented on the com-link, as he stared into the view screen.

"*It is.* I don't have much of a choice not to look at it. Anything *is* possible. We have to divert it. I don't think it's very friendly..."

"There are even *more* mosquito ships flying in! Olin?" Kalantha revealed, checking the radar screen blipping warnings.

Cian glanced to her, then down to the radar screen.

All of a sudden the *Dreadful Flying Glove* encircled them, and went in for the kill, grabbing the flyer within its huge fingered grasp and squeezing it, chomping, starting to crunch on it in mid-air, the insides of the ship started to dent and pucker... the blue fingers and teeth were crunching and chomping and squeezing the ship...

"All right, time to leave, nothing more we can do here now, it will run its course. Hang on..." Cian just calmly voiced.

Olin Cian pulled a manual lever on the left of his seat forcibly, pushing two blue buttons labeled "*Gorm Granna*" while the ship violently shook, the computers frizzed... the view screen started to fuzz out...

"*Hey, Olin Cian! Kalantha! Ringo? Where are you GOING? Your ship, it's getting eaten! Where are you GOING?*"

The view screen fizzed out, as the cockpit around the trio started to break and smoke. Olin unstrapped himself, Ringo and Kalantha. He pulled them closer protectively as Kalantha held onto Ringo and he shielded her as parts on the flyer ceiling crunch and bent about. The Figurines shook their heads and popped back into the pouch.

"This vehicle will self destruct in a few seconds. Timothy, we will meet up again, I just need to tie up some things before that. Enjoy your time with the Uptoppers and lead them well. You know you can do it just as well as I; you know that." Cian encouraged, speaking into the cockpit mike, as the sides of the ship folded and bent in even more...

"Is this *it* for *us?*" Kalantha managed to get out.

"That is our decision. We *ARE* Transporters; Time and space may no longer exist for us." He strongly told her.

"I'm kind of new at this, Olin. I need your help," Kalantha whispered.

"ME TOO! " Ringo whimpered.

"Thank you for asking, lovie. Ok, Ringo, Mate; Keep your concentration and hold your breath... do not let go of me," Cian instructed.

Just as the *Dreadful Blue Flying Glove* smote its killing blow to the flyer, Kalantha, Ringo and Olin Cian started to fade from view within a golden, purple mist...dissipating and altogether vanishing...

The Huge **Blue Dreadful flying glove** snarled in offense and the flyer exploded right in his grasp...blowing him up...

"*All together now*

All together now...
All together now
All to-ge-ther... noooooooow..."

Chapter Ten

A white, shining, shimmery ball of light started to form and solidify into the figures of Olin Cian, Kalantha, and Ringo, who was once again nestled in her arms. What they were forming about and into was a bit confusing to explain... there was a song softly playing in their ears, gentle and subdued...

"Imagine..."

The transporting trio was taking shape into interloping time and space dimensions, yet it was more than just one or two: it was more like four to six different dimensions layered upon on another in transparency, like onion layers, translucent, phantom-like, ghosts upon ghosts of various dimensions and time periods, layers upon layers of specter images and worlds, time eras or dimensions upon and interlocking each other, from the ancient past up to future events, only it was within just one point of view from where they were standing, the akashic records...

The closest one that they were forming into and about to stand upon was a gross dimensional form of a tall, rocky hill with cut stone steps leading behind them to a stone tower, overlooking a deep valley gorge. Other buildings and structures could be seen and were present there, from houses to skyscrapers, but they were all translucent... and from different periods in time. They were seeing everything happening all at once in one focal point from where they were about to be standing.

Once they had solidly formed, Olin stepped forward, encircling his arm about Kalantha's shoulders and pointing outward at the strange, eerie sight of all the worlds within worlds dimensions going on at the same time.

"Imagine there's no heaven
It's easy if you try
No hell below us
Above us only sky...
Imagine all the people living for today
Imagine there's no countries
It isn't hard to do
Nothing to kill or die for
And no religion too
Imagine all the people living life in peace, you
You may say I'm a dreamer
But I'm not the only one
I hope some day you'll join us
And the world will be as one...
Imagine no possessions
I wonder if you can
No need for greed or hunger
A brotherhood of man
Imagine all the people sharing all the world, you
You may say I'm a dreamer
But I'm not the only one
I hope some day you'll join us
And the world will be as one..."

"WE MADE IT, LOVIE. See? There are realms upon realms, Kalantha. All are here for you. I thought that if seeing it like this *first* it might have a better effect for your grasp of how things are for you now.

It will help your perspective. We may go *anywhere,* from the top even to the bottom realms. I'd say they aren't really up or down, back or forth it's just for me to you, some way of describing them. Now, you are at a more advanced stage of practice and development," he softly told her.

Kalantha was just trying to take it all in, looking at it all, the ghost layered realms made her mind blown and she thought she had read up on this kind of stuff and occurrences, but when you *actually have it in front of you,* and seeing it happening, it was a far different story... and unbelievable sensation. She hugged Ringo and breathed out a silent sigh, and it was almost indescribable.

"Am I able to see all this now... due to *you?* **Where** are we?" she softly voiced.

Olin Cian took a step downward on the stone cliff in front of the tower, leading Kalantha over with him.

"It's due to our work *together,* yes, but I don't claim credit for it. We are half through the gross world of matter, and the world of form, the world of "heavens," if you want to label it that. I can show you the "hells" if you wish to call it, some lower realms, denser, yet unwise to lurk down there unless you have specific plans to *help* someone or life form you know there. But... it *can* be done. Look *closely* in the valley below. We can see what is going on there, while in this realm here."

Olin pointed down to the sloping ridge in the ghostly valley gorge below them. It showed a very large, very huge high-tech circular ship, a *yellow one, the size and a half of a football field stadium,* with various people milling about and trying to set up a camp or living area.

The scene sharpened and narrowed as Olin pointed at it, as if a magnifying glass was being placed atop it, showing a better close up view of exactly what was going on, and who it *was.*

It was *Timothy,* overseeing the Uptoppers and crew who had just arrived and starting to form a site to live. Timothy was smiling and actually holding his hands and arms out and forming the earth and dirt and boulders and rocks with his energy and creating solid, useful, massive structures with organic materials to habituate in, just with his pure mind, will, and energy.

The rocks and boulders sailed and formed structures for houses and buildings, fusing together with only his energy and mind. It was as if he was some kind of Merlin magician able to create things from the earth from scratch.

The Uptoppers were all staring at him in disbelief; some of his crew was helping to do it with him, as he aided them in instruction and energy, handing out the Hihiirokane stones, the ones he had picked up to save from the floor after Olin's attack. They were on necklaces like Kalantha's. He was overseeing it all, creating a village and the formula for a city, a mix of very ancient old with the new; he was using Olin Cian's blueprint plan as he had memorized it.

As he did this he kind of stopped a moment, turning his head behind him to stare in Cian and Kalantha's direction vaguely, as if sensing something. A beautiful equine-like creature came up behind him to nuzzle him. He patted it and stared once again, out remotely in Olin, Ringo and Kalantha's direction with a small smile, pausing his work.

"That's *Tim!* I can see Timothy..." Kalantha said, with wonder and amazement at what he was doing.

Cian smiled warmly.

"Yes, yes it is, Captain Sergeant Timothy. He is now backwards in time within the Ulster cycle with the Uptoppers and part of the Network. Amazing it seems, but he *is* there, happy to help out everyone, but still needs *a partner.*"

"Can he see us?" She asked.

"No, but he can sense something, feel us. That's why he turned about. A mighty, titanic heart Timothy has, mighty."

Olin Cian suddenly blinked, then he shuddered, and changed his mood strangely. He became more serious, and wary. Nervous; "Do you *sense* something Kalantha? I DO, and it's not good."

"Yes, I do. It's as if something's *not right*, it's the network members. I can feel it. They are still very angered...and *following* us," Kalantha disturbingly revealed, as Ringo whined.

"On the mark, Kalantha; They want to distract us and stop the plan, but we have more work to do, so much more important work to do."

Kalantha turned to stare at him, shaking her head.

"You will never be free of them, will you?" she whispered, tense and worried.

"Nor will you, but things can *change, they* can change and *evolve back*. Homing devices fail, even if they have them now, and positive feelings will evolve in time for them. I will help them if I can, if they allow me. It can be changed. I've seen it. The Blue Meanies can *and will* coexist with us." He humorously added.

"*Blue Meanies...*" She echoed, with a small little nervous laugh. "I can't believe they are actually *real.*"

Cian turned to look at her, taking her hand in his with a gesture of care.

"You know they were created out of all our own fears and dark thoughts, don't you? They exist only because of what we do and think. They aren't really awful horrible, nothing *is* unless we make it so or is mislead through thoughts and actions to reactions. Everything teaches us to evolve, even our own Tulpas and thought forms that we mistakenly create out of our own minds, positive and negative. They can be friendly...eventually. And *our work* isn't in vain. We are not doing so badly, you know. How are you adjusting to this?"

"I'm getting used to it like I'm getting used to **you.** Is this what you're able see *all the time*?" She mysteriously inquired.

"Quite a bit of it; you can control it if you think upon it. This might be easier."

All at once, the scene before them sharpened and morphed, as if a camera lens was being focused. Kalantha, holding Ringo, and Olin

Cian were now standing atop the deck rim of the tower top archway opening of the *Sherry Netherland Hotel* Building, Fifth Avenue and 59th street, New York City, as the sun was setting.

They were way on top of the spire and near the archway and gargoyles. They stared downward, to a huge panoramic view of the square and park, streets below. The time period was remarkably different, and they saw old 1930's cars and buggies down below. Kalantha gasped, grabbed at the archway opening and held tightly to Ringo and looked out, peering near the railing. Ringo whistled...

Olin Cian mustered a strange smile to Kalantha, and nodded. He peered over the railing and took a glance down. A white dove, a pigeon, landed on the rail next to him.

"Hi there, come for the view?" He said to it, gently. The dove cooed, and ruffled its feathers. He reached out to touch and pet it.

A warped, shaky music tune started to seep through... it was that strange, darkened **Eleanor Rigby Dub step** version once more...

Dark, smoky blue spirals started to wind around the archway openings behind Kalantha and Ringo, and *then seized them...* and entwined all about their forms like a jellyfish...

Cian, caught off guard, whirled around to see the sight...

"NO! Kalantha! Ringo!"

The smoky swirls of light ensnared Kalantha and Ringo entirely, pulling them upward and outward, off the building and into the air...Olin Cian grabbed Kalantha's hand as she struggled to free herself and speak. Ringo yelped, snapping his teeth at the dark blue tendrils, squeezing them...

"It's the council members it has to be! The Meanies, they're trying to pull us back! I don't know if I can hold them off, I'm too weak, and tired," her muffled voice faltered as she fought to get free.

$\times$

"I AM SENDING YOU MY energy..." Olin nervously told her, concentrating.

"YOU *need* your energy, Olin! I'll *try* to transport to get us out of it! *Help me,* help me do it," she barely got out, as the tentacles wrapped about her, Ringo, and her mouth...

Bursts of silver light streamed forth from Olin Cian's chest area, to Kalantha's chest like a connective cord. Eerie, echoing laughs of the Meanies permeated the area; Kalantha and Ringo started to fade into golden specks of light... smaller, smaller, until nothing was left, and the shadowy blue tendrils that had held them melted off,... and away.

Olin Cian heaved a heavy, broken emotive sigh, full of pain and abandonment, and held on to the railing for sheer support, drained. He slowly lifted his head to stare out remotely. The wind began to pick up as the dark dub step music... stopped, as did the laughter. He took a few, deep breaths and calmed down, feeling out for any inkling of Kalantha and Ringo's whereabouts.

"You're *both ok,* you *made it.* I know where you *are.* Hopefully you'll wait there," his soft voice spoke, more at peace.

Cian looked to the dove, then outward, as if towards *"us"* with a contrite smile, as if he was apologizing for everything. The dove hopped onto his shoulder. He stared over at it and gave a nod, and he disappeared within violet golden specs of light...

Chapter Eleven

The beautiful, warm spring day in Central Park was in high gear. You would say it was just as gorgeous as the previous one when Kalantha had gone home mumbling about her hand.

It was now mid afternoon, and park goers were park going near the large fountain area on the shore of the boathouse lake, Bethesda Terrace. Some crazy street clown was blowing huge, billowing bubbles on the red brick walkway, entertaining the children brought in by their nannies; the tourists were snapping photos, using their selfie sticks.

It was late spring break week for many of the public school kids, and a whole high school group of them had decided to hang out near the area, near the edge of the lake and were sitting on some stone benches built into the edge. They were fiddling with their phones, and one of them turned up the volume to a song they had turned on...

"When I'm Sixty-Four"...

CROUCHING DOWN NEAR the lake edge where there was no stone barrier, Kalantha was sitting, staring out at the boaters rowing oars. There were many couples out today, even a few who had just married and still in their bride and groom attire, taking a once around the lake for romance's sake.

She huddled herself even closer to Ringo, who was nestled quite nicely in her lap, the cylinder with the plans still slung over her shoulder. She had been there, sitting there and had "appeared" there

174

since dawn when no one was even about and had stayed put for deep in her heart it told her to; The high school kids had been watching her since mid-morning, staring at her rather interesting dress, for it looked like a movie costume. It was a lovely garment and very unique. She sighed deeply and bowed her head, almost about to cry.

The music from the student's phone seemed to grow louder... actually, it had randomly hooked up to Olin Cian's built in speaker system which hadn't been officially used just yet, at least not in this day and time, but secretly existed and had been there for years,... and it did so automatically, so the song just started to boom out...

Everyone started and looked about, smiling, thinking there was a concert about to start in the old bandstand behind the stone steps and bridge archway. Kalantha also twitched and started; for she knew only *one person* could actually be the reason *for* it.

"When I get older, losing my hair,
Many years from now
Will you still be sending me a Valentine
Birthday greetings bottle of wine?
If I'd been out till quarter to three
Would you lock the door,
Will you still need me, will you still feed me,
When I'm sixty-four?
You'll be older too,
And if you say the word,
I could stay with you
I could be handy, mending a fuse
When your lights have gone
You can knit a sweater by the fireside
Sunday mornings go for a ride,
Doing the garden, digging the weeds,
Who could ask for more
Will you still need me, will you still feed me,

When I'm sixty-four?
Every summer we can rent a cottage,
In the Isle of Wight, if it's not too dear
We shall scrimp and save
Grandchildren on your knee
Vera, Chuck and Dave
Send me a postcard, drop me a line
Stating point of view
Indicate precisely what you mean to say
Yours sincerely, wasting away
Give me your answer, fill in a form
Mine for evermore
Will you still need me, will you still feed me
When I'm sixty-four..."

KALANTHA STARTED AND stood up, turning towards where the music was coming from, seeming somewhere to her left behind her... she wasn't sure. The group of teenagers that had been watching her started to walk over to her. Ringo also had jumped off her lap and perked up at the music.

"Did you... happen to *lose someone*? Kinda had a fight or something?" One of the guy teens asked, curiously.

"Did I-? Yes, yes I did," she softly said back to them oddly, wondering how they-

"That's a really cool dress, we're askin' 'cause, well, we didn't see him but one of our friends saw this dude-he's kinda dressed up a little, um, like *you are* and they told us about him," a girl told her, fiddling with her smartphone. The phone, it then started blaring out another tune simultaneously as the other music with Cian's stereo system ebbed out... she blinked and almost dropped it...

It blared out the fluted first notes of a very familiar song...

"Strawbery Fields..."

Ringo heard it and bolted, started scampering as fast as his paws could go; Kalantha followed, not too far behind him, out of the fountain area and down the paths, the group of teens also in pace with them not wanting to miss this one because it sure seemed to be interesting to them... Kalantha and Ringo knew exactly where they were running off to... it wasn't very far. The song continued banging out as they ran.

"Let me take you down
'Cause I'm going to Strawberry Fields
Nothing is real
And nothing to get hung about
Strawberry Fields forever
Living is easy with eyes closed
Misunderstanding all you see
It's getting hard to be someone
But it all works out
It doesn't matter much to me
Let me take you down
'Cause I'm going to Strawberry Fields
Nothing is real
And nothing to get hung about
Strawberry Fields forever..."

As Ringo and Kalantha and their tag along group finally made it there, to Strawberry Fields in Central Park, everyone around the area was trying to figure out just where the music was coming from. The musicians there that would hang out weren't playing just now. It just seemed to "hover" right over the area, right over the memorial mosaic on the pavement, the "Imagine" mosaic with its flowers and mementos.

Someone was bending down on the side of it, placing a live white dove there, someone wearing the same kind of clothes Kalantha had on.

Kalantha and Ringo stopped short, breathless, on the other side of the memorial opposite of him.

Olin Cian quietly stood back up. On his eyes he had on his pair of round, iridescent, psychedelic sunglasses. Then, he and Kalantha both walked slowly over to each other, Ringo with them, in front of the mosaic on the ground, the only ones not freaking out by the music... the only ones who knew what was going on.

The group of students noticed him and murmured, and the teen girl with the phone with the song that started it did a double take at him, and her phone.

Cian reached out, and touched Kalantha's shoulder lightly. Her reaction turned from sorrow to utter joy and relief. Ringo made a surprised sound.

"Hi, lovie," he softly told her, warmly, the music also giving him away.

Kalantha threw her arms about him, smiling. Ringo jumped up and down, wagging his tail, and all the park-goers reacted to their embrace, whistling, thinking it was one of those staged scenes of street performers paid for by the Park Dept. and Delacorte Theatre.

The Figurines popped their heads out of Kalantha's pouch and laughed, giving each other a high five before diving back in. One of the teen boys took a step towards them.

"You know, she's been sitting all the way over there almost *all day* before we even showed up, and we've been around since nine a.m. *and* it's now three p.m. What, did you two have a fight or something? At least you brought a peace offering." He gestured toward the dove. "You going to kiss her and make up? I don't see any flowers or chocolate? They LIKE those, you know, and concert or movie tickets or makeup, or an album, some kind of clothes or games, jewelry," The teen guy commented, looking him over, intrigued at his clothing, his "threads," for he was a design student. He kind of liked them, then glanced upward trying to find the music speakers if there were any.

Cian looked to the group of teenagers, then to Kalantha, rather even shyly.

"Well, I-I'm kind of emancipated, enlightened. Uh-um-it took a while to get here, didn't have time to stop and-" he got out, brokenly.

"Whah? *Whut?* Bro, that has to be the funniest and weirdest excuse YET," he remarked, shaking his head and staring at him strangely, then up at the echoing music... "Must be a concert going on somewhere in the Park, it's pretty loud."

"Did you get that answer from the Jerry Springer show or Maury? OMG, Male minds!" The teen girl with the phone sarcastically commented, in a very distinctive voice.

"Oh, no, no, you see I truly love her, see I-we-

"Ah, cool, it's fine. We see you got matching outfits together, cool," another teen boy cut him off. "Nice suit, must've cost a fortune, the new thing to do I guess. Your girl here she's got some kind of engineering plans with her. Are you building something? We all go to High School of Art and Design here in Manhattan. Those plans look interesting." The young man leaned over and stared at the see-thru blueprints in Kalantha's cylinder.

"She ain't *your girl?*" The teen girl with the distinctive voice and phone declared.

Olin Cian started to laugh softly, but stopped it and smiled, shaking his head.

"Kalantha and I-we have known each other a long time," he explained.

"Oh, now really? *Really?* Then that's a definite reason to kiss her, and the right way. I see. You show up with a dove on your shoulder, give it to Strawberry Fields AND a matching outfit AND say all these things that you LOVE HER then that she isn't *your girl?* That's messed.

OKAY, just okay, do it once, you need to, that's all it takes you know. Honestly," the teen girl with the phone huffed to him.

All the students then stared at him, waiting. Olin Cian then looked over at Kalantha, and down at Ringo who was starting to giggle, knowing he was at an impasse with this group.

"If I do, will you listen to me for a while? I can show you my plans, those plans. I think you'd really like to see them being design students, even help me out with them. I'm in need of some expert, really good help. Besides, I didn't even get to feel it last time I kissed her, and then she told me *not to* the *second* time I asked her." Cian pressed, complaining ridiculously.

Kalantha made this incredible soured face and tried not to laugh.

"Well, ok yeah, sure, I'm interested. We'll listen and take a look. I can see a bit of it through that cylinder. You two are... different. We get it. You must be foreigners." The young man next to the girl earnestly replied.

Olin Cian turned towards the teen girl with the phone, at a loss, but trying to explain himself to her.

"Um, sorry, I don't know if I'll feel anything if I-I-um-

"If you KISS her? *If you kiss her?* WHAT? Didn't get to FEEL it the *last time?* And how did that by chance happen? You do her justice; you've known her a long time! You're gonna FEEL something all right! OH GOD, so lame, men are unbelievable. Sixty percent of your heart is made of BRAIN cells, so I'm SURE *something* is gonna be felt and connected there, geez!" she exasperated, pointing her finger at him.

Cian raised his eyebrow at her, and tilted his head, taking off his sunglasses to stare at her intently.

"*Clorinde?*" He questioned.

"Um,... *Yeah, that's me,* that's **my name...** do we *know* each other?" She paused, glaring at him for she had gotten to get a good look at his face without the sunglasses. "***OH, no, Wait a minute...***"

She studied him a moment. Then her hand flew to her mouth in freaked astonishment.

"*Oh, God you*-you're *Jeremy Hilary Bube!* The missing kid with the musician parents... You went to *our* High school some years back, almost about seven years ago I think. They all said you... just *vanished*. No one could figure or find a trace of you, not your family, the school, or the cops. You were a *top design student,* Jeremy. They have all of your awards and a huge framed photo poster of you in a cabinet in the hallway of the school when you walk into the lobby like some memorial. Everyone in school knows of you, even have a scholarship named after you. They all think you were taken off, or mugged and thrown into the docks or something, missing on the milk carton or news material. *Everyone in that school knows who you are, or were.* You don't look much different, just a bit "rugged." *What the hell happened to you?* You're **BACK?** It's been *years!*"

The students all gave each other strange, pausing glances, also recognizing him, then just stared back at him, mesmerized, waiting for him to say something.

Olin Cian silently stared over at the students, making a caught face, kind of holding in a laugh, unable to explain it all in one sentence or even two; Then he dipped Kalantha, giving her a nice, lovely kiss, a long, dramatic one, Hollywood style.

A pink-gold auric light emanated forth from them, sparkling, shimmering, at least ten feet or more. The students and everyone about the memorial all squealed and vocally reacted in awe and shock. Some further out onlookers thought it was a park magic show and clapped, catching the glitter with their hands. Ringo turned his head and hid his eyes with his paw, embarrassed.

"What the-oh man, oh damn this is better than the movies This is REAL! You are REAL. Who the hell ARE you? *Are you Jeremy?* Clorinde recognized you!" The young man got out, trying to touch the shimmery pink lights. Another crowd of people started to walk over towards them, seeing the shiny pink lights, murmuring, the music and the song replaying again...

Olin Cian stopped kissing Kalantha, pulled her back up and addressed his newfound crew.

"Let's just say, ah, some Blue Meanies held me up for a ...while. I must admit that Kiss was pretty brilliant, lovely. I forgot what it felt like. I'm Olin, Olin Cian. Well, that's what they all call me NOW, my colleagues re-named me where I was at, um, said the name I had just didn't suit me; The Uptoppers said I should go undercover, a bit of a change but yes, my real name... *is* Jeremy Hilary Bube, and this, is Kalantha. The truth is always waiting, just up to you to find it."

"He's the Nowhere Man. Ahem (Cough) you always forget ME." Ringo commented.

The crowd grew silent in strange strangled shock, glaring at Ringo. He just giggled again, wagging his tail.

"A thousand apologies; This is my best friend, Ringo. Sorry about the music, it just decides to come with us wherever we go because I forgot to turn it off at... home. And I kind of can't get back there just now, not for a while. Maybe tonight, but it never really turns off... it isn't about to now, it helps with the Blue Meanies, you know. They're on their way," Olin truthfully apologized. "Clorinde, we may even have some time for a game of...*chess.* I really like that little portable set you carry around with you."

He winked to her.

Clorinde gaped at him, and at Ringo.

Checking her backpack, she opened it and swiftly pulled out a new, little wooden chess set box, glaring down at it, then to him.

The students were dumbfounded at a talking dog, and just about everything else they had just seen and heard. They all started asking questions at once, surrounding them, and a larger crowd started to walk over to them, pointing... excited, interested, amazed ... a couple of cops were there too but they just started to back off...

"No one I think is in my tree
I mean it must be high or low
That is you can't, you know, tune in
But it's all right
That is, I think, it's not too bad
Let me take you down
'Cause I'm going to Strawberry Fields
Nothing is real
And nothing to get hung about
Strawberry Fields forever..."

"It sure looks like I have my work cut out for me, lovie. You know it's going to start all over now, and we might have time to change it, with a little help from our friends. Listen, Timothy's *waiting*... for *YOU*," Cian whispered to Kalantha, over all the commotion. "I *need* to spend a bit of time with **them.** Tim's a fun guy, you know he is, you'll love it. He's been waiting just as long as I have for you but he'd never tell you, much too shy. I told you he needs a *partner.* He fell in love with you at *first sight*, you know. I'll pop in from time to time, and we'll see how it all works out. And, then it'll start all over again, next time around will not be as bad, you'll see. Let's go!"

"Always, no, sometimes think it's me
But you know I know when it's a dream
I think, er, no, I mean, er, yes
But it's all wrong
That is I think I disagree
Let me take you down
'Cause I'm going to Strawberry Fields
Nothing is real
"And nothing to get hung about
Strawberry Fields forever
Strawberry Fields forever
Strawberry Fields forever..."

CIAN TURNED, TO LOOK outward, once again, kind of towards *"us"* - and winked, smiled broadly once more, then nudged Kalantha to turn.

She turned about to see what he was looking at, and so did Ringo, who smiled and laughed, jumping into Kalantha's arms.

The Figurines popped out of her pouch, tugged on Kalantha's dress sleeve, and also winked at her. Kalantha's eyes grew large, and she shook her head, blushing and laughed a bit, finally seeing what Cian had always been able to see and understand all along:

US.

"Cranberry Sauce"... ended the song.

A blare of trumpets in the breeze echoed, as if the heavens opened up, which heralded *another all too familiar* song just as Olin Cian tapped his foot on the front part of the mosaic of the memorial....

A purple-blue shaft of shimmery light encompassed the students and them all, and they all dematerialized... while on top of the memorial... Olin Cian's round iridescent sunglasses fell down onto the middle of the Imagine mosaic, the only visible thing left...

The dove settled down next to the glasses, cooing the three notes of the song about to play. All the park onlookers glared over at it, and each other, bewildered and stunned, listening to the song now wafting over the skies as they clambered over to where Olin, Kalantha, Ringo and the students had vanished, examining the area in mystery, caution, and ponderous shock...

"ALL YOU NEED IS LOVE"...

"Love, Love, Love.
Love, Love, Love.
Love, Love, Love.

There's nothing you can do that can't be done.
Nothing you can sing that can't be sung.
Nothing you can say but you can learn how to play the game.
It's easy.
Nothing you can make that can't be made.
No one you can save that can't be saved.
Nothing you can do but you can learn how to be you in time.
It's easy.
All you need is love.
All you need is love.
All you need is love, love.
Love is all you need.
Nothing you can know that isn't known.
Nothing you can see that isn't shown.
Nowhere you can be that isn't where you're meant to be.
It's easy..."

THE SPINNING, WINDING vortex of the spiraling energy wormhole of light that Kalantha holding Ringo in her arms experienced slowed down, and she was now materializing...

The song, however, stuck with them...

Captain Sergeant Timothy Ban Piobar was sitting crouched in front of a crackling bonfire on a hand-woven mat, cooking in a caldron in the evening dusk lighting. Some herbs and chopped veggies hovered on top of the vegetarian brew, Timothy using his special transporting "skill" even to pick up the ingredients to his bubbling stew, then plopping them in.

There was an equine–type creature somewhat resembling a horse/giraffe as before grazing behind him, swishing its tail, and some black and white "cow" type creatures, but their faces were not that of a cow. Behind them were some newly formed stone cottages, teepees, and large tents included in with some elaborate futuristic formed residences and structures, lots of rolling hills and psychedelic oddities seeming very familiar... It was a mix of the very ancient and high future architecture, as well as resembling in real life... Talamh Piobar...*Pepperland... it was turning into Pepperland*...if you could describe it, strangely psychedelic but live cartoon...everything was beginning to take shape...only with Celtic accents.

Timothy had been forming it all day with his energies. On a raised stone stepped platform that he had built, as in Pepperland, now Talamh Piobar, in the distance, on top stood the huge, spectacular, circular, yellow flying ship submarine, a carved sentence in the boulders fused together by Timothy for a docking port, looking down upon it all bearing a sign beneath it:

"*TALAMH PIOBAR, #2*".

Various Uptoppers were getting ready for the night in the city village. Some were still dancing and creating revelry, trying to corral the weird "creatures" of Talamh Piobar #2, organic manifestations of the "cartoon" animals and creatures of the Yellow Submarine storyline; but most were hunkering down for the evening. They stopped what they were doing, waving at Timothy and bowing. He waved back at them, bowing back in reverence and honor to them. He then turned back and poked at the fire with a stick, a bit solemn, very quiet, checking his bubbling stew.

Then he heard the tune that was melodiously wafting in... getting stronger and louder... without any amplifier system at all, and with curiosity he anticipated... just wondered, truly heart fully **hoped-** and then, dreamily, wishfully turned his head towards the sound of it,...in amazed confounded intrigue.

"*Love Is All You Need...*"

Kalantha, who was clutching Ringo, materialized right in front of Timothy.

He gazed up, upon her and stood slowly, golden almond eyes glinting, not believing what was joyously before him. His eyelashes started to get wet. He shyly moved over to both of them and silently, because he didn't need to say a thing, he just softly reached over and hugged Kalantha and Ringo, as the pink, auric sparkling lights shot out everywhere like sun rays as he contacted them, overcome with emotion.

Ringo let out a wolf whistle. The Figurines, they hopped out of Kalantha's pouch, climbing upon her arm, winking, waving, shoving each other, play fighting on her shoulder, then pointing up to her.

"*Love is all you need...*" Ringo whispered, sang and giggled out to **US**, as some funky balled collar and polka dot pant clothing started forming upon him, and a funny hat, the end of his tail morphing in and out as a drum pound stick...for if you check or knew the icon, you'd see a pooch like him in front of the big drum from Sgt. Pepper's Band in Pepperland; Timothy, the big softie that he was, moved in closer slowly to kiss Kalantha...

"*All you need is love (All together, now!)*
All you need is love (Everybody!)
All you need is love, love. Love is all you need (love is all you need)..."

Love is all you need...

THE END

Don't miss out!

Visit the website below and you can sign up to receive emails whenever Laura Jean Lysander publishes a new book. There's no charge and no obligation.

https://books2read.com/r/B-A-LOIF-RWEAB

BOOKS 2 READ

Connecting independent readers to independent writers.

Did you love *Nowhere Man: Transporter*? Then you should read *Universally Yours, The Phoenix* by Laura Jean Lysander!

2nd Edition ~ Introducing Jonathan Gold; he was humorous, happy-go-lucky, super-athletic, unusually handsome and warm-hearted; he naively thought he had it made, he thought everything was pulling together for his college future, going his way; soon to be decorated high school Sports Grad, class of 1982, those fabulous football scholarships kept coming in for the asking, all at his taking lining up, maybe even a great job at the Gym/Dojo he belonged to; it seemed ridiculous; how could something like this actually happen to him?

He, with all his martial arts trophy training and unheard of glorified health, how could he be shockingly shanghaied, subdued and shafted from his own bedroom in the middle of the night without being able to defend himself? Well, it sure did happen, and to him.

And then, waking up in a floppy fog, to see a husky, hulking, hairy kidnapper Bruce and his lovely latino-looking lady doctor Sheila, his cohort asking him such odd nonsensical personal questions? Was it just some haphazard undercover mix-up, a big, glaring mistake? It gets even stranger for him when he winds up once more waking up after a harrowing, burning ring caper to see the most gorgeous gal, Selene, staring down at him, one with such beautiful violet-hued eyes and platinum hair, just as he had? Was it just a dream?

Yet what they were being told about themselves by these mysterious abductors made it even more bizarre- and it takes an even more unbelievable turn when they are forced to take a very far, far away trip- and Jon wakes up even again somewhere else... with a funky piece of feather-light, haloed jewelry on his neck and some tunes and lyrics blaring that begins to change his entire life forever...

Also by Laura Jean Lysander

SARDOODLEDOM

Sardoodledom: The Broken Rule Part One
Sardoodledom: The Broken Rule Part One
Darkened Promise
Darkened Promise Part Two
Darkened Promise
Darkened Promise Part Two

Standalone

Nowhere Man, Transporter
Nowhere Man, Transporter
Universally Yours, The Phoenix
Universally Yours, The Phoenix
In Your Dreams
In Your Dreams
Nowhere Man: Transporter